"What's wrong?"

In the faint light of the bedroom, Chris's expression looked sheepish. "Uh, we need to stop. In my rush to get here, I didn't have a chance to take care of things."

He wanted to stop? What for...? Oh.

"It's okay," Rei assured him. "I have protection in my purse."

Chris grinned at her. "You really did think I was a sure thing, didn't you?"

She shrugged while returning his smile. "I was feeling unusually confident when I called you, so..."

"So hurry up and get that condom."

Rei rolled off the bed and scrambled for her handbag. Within seconds she'd returned to the bed and tossed several strips of foil packages onto the comforter. Chris looked at her, then at the dozen condoms and back at her.

"Your confidence is going to kill me for sure."

Responding to the humor in his voice, she laughed. "Maybe. But what a way to go, huh?"

Blaze™

Dear Reader,

The original title of this story was *You've Got Male* because I wanted to explore the phenomenon of e-mail communication and online dating. But, as often happens to me, the lighthearted romp I had in mind segued into an exploration of how to find and accept love.

Neither Rei Davis nor Chris London believes in love. They don't trust that it will last, and think "happily ever after" is only for other people. At least, until they find each other. With the help of instant messages, a fantasy brought to life and a few leaps of faith, both of their wishes will come true, because love and forgiveness have the power to heal.

I wish you happy reading and I wish you joy,

Mia

P.S. You can contact me via my Web site, www.miazachary.com. I'd love to hear from you.

AUTHOR'S NOTE

A portion of my royalties from sales of this book will be donated to the Susan G. Komen Breast Cancer Foundation.

Books by Mia Zachary

HARLEQUIN BLAZE
83—RED SHOES & A DIARY
136—YOURS IN BLACK LACE
160—9 1/2 DAYS

AFTERNOON DELIGHT
Mia Zachary

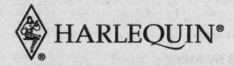

HARLEQUIN®

TORONTO • NEW YORK • LONDON
AMSTERDAM • PARIS • SYDNEY • HAMBURG
STOCKHOLM • ATHENS • TOKYO • MILAN • MADRID
PRAGUE • WARSAW • BUDAPEST • AUCKLAND

To Wayne

Heartfelt gratitude goes to my creative writing partner,
Melissa James. Thank you for helping me open the door to the
past and for holding my hand while I walked through it.

ISBN 0-373-79251-4

AFTERNOON DELIGHT

This edition published by arrangement with Harlequin Books S.A.

® and TM are trademarks of the publisher. Trademarks indicated with
® are registered in the United States Patent and Trademark Office, the
Canadian Trade Marks Office and in other countries.

www.eHarlequin.com

Printed in U.S.A.

1

TO: Rei Davis <RL_Davis@UFC.sf.gov>
FR: Phoebe J. Hollinger <PJH@hhfs.com>
RE: Are you busy?
If you don't already have plans with Darren tonight, do you want to get together?
P.J.

Hollinger/Hansen: San Francisco, Tokyo, London, New York
Diversified Financial Services, Individual Client Commitment
TO: Phoebe J. Hollinger <PJH@hhfs.com>
FR: Rei Davis <RL_Davis@UFC.sf.gov>
RE: Tonight
I don't have any plans. Derek took me to The Top of the Mark last night. (Keep your I-told-you-so to yourself, though. The irony that was not lost on me.)
I finally broke up with him. (Keep your I-never-liked-him-anyway to yourself, too.)
Rei

Unified Family Court, 400 McAllister Street, San Francisco
All kids need is a little help, a little hope and somebody who believes in them. —Earvin "Magic" Johnson

RE: Single again
I told you The Mark was a weird choice for a date. That's where sailors had their last drink before shipping out to the Pacific in WWII.
Well, I'm sorry it's over but, hell, I never liked Derek anyway. Like the other men you've chosen, he was opinionated, self-righteous and argumentative. You shouldn't date lawyers.
When are you going to admit that I'm always right?
P.J.

RE: Already over it
Nice ego there, honey. You should have that checked.
And I told you not to say I told you!
I'm not as sorry as maybe I should be. Then again, it's not like we were serious.
Rei

RE: You can't be serious
Never had sex with him, huh?
I think one of our Break Away Nights is in order. I heard about this new place, Divas. Thursday night is Ladies Night so there's bound to be great people

(by that I mean men-who-are-not-lawyers) for you to meet. I'll pick you up at your house at nine.
P.J.

RE: Break Away Night
Is that my nine or your nine? Because my nine is actually nine, whereas your nine usually means ten. So why don't we say eight? That way we'll both be on time.
Recess is almost over. See you later.
Rei

SUPERIOR COURT Commissioner Rei Davis clicked the button to send the message to her best friend then signed out of her e-mail program. Turning her chair, she gazed out the small grimy window to the French Renaissance facade of the War Memorial Opera House across Van Ness Avenue. She'd never actually been to an opera or even listened to one to find out if she liked it. Something else to add to her *Life List*.

Life. The word had a wonderful feel, one that spread through her like bright rays of sunlight through cloud. She'd just gone for her checkup with Dr. Solís this past Monday, April seventh, one year to the day.... She was blessed to still be alive and she knew it.

As she heard the outer door to her chambers open, she turned to see Mary Alice, her court services clerk. The petite older woman held an armful of case files, a harried expression on her kind face. "They're ready for you, Commissioner. Five walk-ins were just added to the docket, including a case that was transferred from Judge Shuford."

She schooled her expression, repressing a sigh. She'd already handled thirteen cases before calling a recess for lunch. Now the afternoon caseload would either run late or have to be rescheduled.

"All right, thanks. I'll be right in."

Once upon a time, she really had been quicktempered and over-ambitious, an impatient and obsessively ambitious corporate law attorney who treated everything in her life like a merger or acquisition. Then she'd discovered a lump in her right breast that irrevocably changed her life...

Despite a partnership being well within reach, she had quit her lucrative position with the law firm. Instead she'd accepted a position as a referee, a Family Court officer appointed by the presiding judge to hear cases that involved juveniles. She'd been given a second chance and wanted to make a difference in the lives of others. She'd thrown herself into the job and three months later applied for one of the vacant Court Commissioner slots.

Family was the thread that wove together the fabric of society, the backbone of civilization. On a good day, she was proud to help maintain the family structure by approving adoptions, resolving custody disputes and returning kids in foster care to their homes.

Lately, however, she felt tired and disillusioned. The docket before her made it easy to believe the backbone of civilization was twisted and crumbling beneath the weight of crime, abuse and neglect. There were too many days when she felt like all she could do was shovel sand against the surge. But life was precious, especially the life of a child who had so much ahead if only someone gave them a chance.

Rei pushed away from the desk and stood up, brushing a hand over her chignon, and reached for the black robe hanging on her coat rack. Squaring her shoulders, she mentally prepared herself to tilt at some windmills and try to turn a few tides.

"VISITATION IS HEREBY revoked pending the Defendant's completion of both anger management and substance abuse programs. Mrs. Landis will continue to have full custody of the children."

"You can't do this! You can't take my kids away from me!"

"I just did, Mr. Landis." Rei spoke sharply and frowned at the alcoholic who thought it was okay to strike his sons with a beer bottle. "We'll reexamine this matter in three months. But for now, we're done here."

"I'm their father and I can damn well discipline my boys when they need it. You're not taking my kids!"

Gathering the case files off the bench, Rei briefly glanced at Landis while a bailiff forcibly removed him from the courtroom. He didn't deserve those kids. Or more to the point, those kids didn't deserve him. Ignoring the empty threats echoing from the hall, she called the next case, *Cannon v. Ogilvy.*

"Mr. Willette, am I reading this file correctly?"

Rei shot a baleful look at the young attorney standing before her. "You're bringing charges of stalking and harassment?"

"That's right, Your Honor. My client, Cindy Cannon, told her parents that James Ogilvy has been following her around and won't leave her alone."

"Your client is six years old, Mr. Willette, and so is the Defendant." She scowled at the child's mother. "I can't believe you're wasting the Court's time with this."

Mrs. Cannon, a prissy brunette with rigid features, stood up and wrung her hands. "Cindy talks about this boy all the time. She says he trails after her on the playground, tries to sit next to her at lunch and hides notes in her book bag."

"That would be exhibits one through five, Your Honor."

Rei held up the multi-colored sheets of construction paper. "You mean these crayon drawings of hearts and smiley faces, Mr. Willette?"

Defense counsel stood as well, but Rei held up one palm before she could speak. "Don't bother, Ms. Schaefer. I'm on it.

She slid the "love letters" back into the file and shut it with a snap. "What we have here, people, is a case of very innocent, very normal, puppy love between elementary school children. Nothing more. Mrs. Cannon, I'm sure there are plenty of women at St. Francis Hospital who could clue you in about what stalking really is. I suggest you get a grip on reality. Case dismissed. What's next?"

"Good afternoon, Commissioner Davis. Frank Dowd, Assistant State's Attorney." He smoothed his tie. "Bruce Grayson is accused of viciously beating an elderly storeowner during the course of an attempted robbery."

Rei glanced over at the child slouched in a chair beside his lawyer. Bruce still had the chubby-faced appearance of a young boy, but his sullen expression and ancient eyes told another, too familiar story. Did happy childhoods only exist in movies and wishful thinking anymore?

"Jeffrey Bates for the Defense, Your Honor. Bruce is only twelve years old. He comes from a broken home, has been in and out of foster care—"

Dowd interrupted. "Yeah, yeah, we all know the heart-breaking story."

Rei tapped her gavel. "Watch it, counselor."

"Sorry, Your Honor. But due to the severity of Mr. Patterson's injuries, as well as Mr. Grayson's priors, the State feels he should be tried as an adult."

"Incarceration in an adult facility will only turn Bruce into a hardened criminal." Bates held up a file. "Our psych eval—"

This time Rei interrupted him. "Hold it, gentlemen. This is going to take longer than we have." Thursday was one of the two days reserved for short cause matters—the cases had to be heard in less than twenty minutes—and Fridays were reserved for adoptions. She looked over at her clerk. "We'll reconvene…"

"Monday at nine thirty," Mary Alice interjected.

"Monday at nine thirty. Thank you, until then."

Rei felt a tug in her gut as she watched the boy swagger out of the courtroom, shoulders squared and expression unrepentant. The postponement meant a few more nights in juvenile hall, but she had to have time to study his record and evaluations and hear all the facts surrounding the case.

At best he'd spend the next six years in a California Youth Authority camp. At worst he would only be in CYA until he turned sixteen then be sent to the Department of Corrections. She hoped she could find a spark of redemption in Bruce Grayson before it was too late. She hated putting children behind bars, no matter what they'd done.

Shuffling the Grayson case aside, Rei called the next matter. Break Away Night couldn't start soon enough.

"WELCOME TO Lunch Meetings," Christopher London warmly greeted his fourth potential client of the morning. He held out a hand but kept his voice low to protect her privacy. "Thank you for choosing us to help enhance your love life."

Tina Farrell, a conventionally attractive redhead, shook his hand and glanced about. "I bet you hear it all the time, but really, I never did anything like this before."

"We realize it's a big step. Most people meet via their family, friends or jobs and, if it doesn't work out, there may be some guilt or pressure as a result.

Here at Lunch Meetings, we try to make dating a fun, friendly and stress-free experience."

She visibly relaxed and sent him a grateful smile. "Glad to hear it."

"Why don't I take your coat and show you around?" Chris hung her jacket in the cloakroom then offered the tumbler of spring water the hostess handed him. "Behind this smoked glass wall is the main dining room, which is open from ten a.m. until three in the afternoon."

Tina's blue eyes widened. "Wow. The place is packed. Is everybody in there on dates?"

"No, the food itself has actually garnered some nice reviews, so a lot of people come just for lunch. That's why we have tables for four as well as for two." He gently took her elbow and guided her along the passageway. "This smaller dining room was designed with all booths for more personal encounters."

"So you're only open during the day?" Tina took a sip of water as she followed beside him.

"We have special events one night a week for our clients, usually just a casual mixer, and we hold formal parties on Valentine's and New Year's Eve."

Tina set her glass down on a side table, challenging him with a look. "What about having to pay extra to be included in events and expensive trips."

"You don't have to worry about that here. I'll give you a membership breakdown that explains exactly what we do and how much it'll cost." Chris gestured toward the inviting area as they walked through. "This is where we hold the parties."

"It's really beautiful. And you've got a stage for live music." She ran a finger along the aged mahogany bar. "Can I come to this week's mixer?"

"Sorry, you missed it already. But, if you decide to sign up for our services, I'll add you to the guest list for next time."

"Oh, I've mostly decided," Tina informed him with laugh. "One of my coworkers went on seven dates with the same man in the past month. She highly recommended you."

"Great. A big percentage of our business comes by word of mouth." Chris smiled and pointed to the framed photographs on the walls. "We've had a lot of success in the two years since we opened. At last count I've been invited to about thirty-five weddings."

"It might be thirty-six soon. My coworker and her boyfriend seem pretty serious already."

He nodded, not surprised. "We put a lot of time, effort and research into our matchmaking program. The key is finding compatible core traits and vital attributes. This enables us to create a portrait of who you are at a deeper level, unlike other services that match people based on photographs and a fictional paragraph."

She clapped her hands together once. "Okay, I'm ready."

"Then let's get started on the paperwork." Chris widened his smile and swept an arm toward his office across the hall. "To your left is the computer café where clients fill out the personality profile and check their LM e-mail accounts. I'll take you inside when we're done."

He waited for Tina to precede him into the office and held the guest chair for her before rounding his desk. After filling a new water glass from the pitcher on the credenza, he reached into one of the file drawers for a new client packet.

"Here are the brochures about the company, about the best ways to present yourself in person and protect yourself online, and some testimonials from former clients. Also in that folder are the application, payment options and an inquiry consent form."

Tina's brow furrowed. "You're going to investigate me?"

"As a precaution, we look into *all* of our applicants' pasts, searching for criminal records. We wouldn't want to accidentally put a client into a dangerous situation." Chris leaned forward to point to a particular paper. "This sheet is the confidentiality statement, basically stating that none of your personal information will ever be revealed or sold to advertisers."

He settled back in his chair, allowing Tina a few minutes to examine the brochures. There was no need to continue his sales pitch—he had good instincts. He recognized the signs of excitement and anticipation that love might be only a few dates away.

Tina looked up from reading. "Are you one of the

'intelligent, dynamic people who are ready to find the love of their life'?"

Chris forced a chuckle. "I'm flattered, but unfortunately not available."

She smiled shyly. "Too bad. You seem like a really nice guy and I like your honesty. She's lucky, your lady."

Honesty was a tightrope he carefully balanced on every day. He hadn't lied—he never dated clients—but he sure as hell hadn't told the whole truth either. He couldn't afford to.

Tina stacked the brochures and closed the folder. "Sounds too good to be true, Chris, but sign me up anyway!"

"Once you fill out all of the forms, I'll take you into the café and show you how to start the questionnaires."

Twenty minutes later, he was back in his office with a capocollo and Swiss on sourdough. He pushed aside the mail his office manager, Lara, had left for him to make room for the sandwich, chips and soda. Lunch Meetings had become known for entrées like spinach, mushroom and chicken quesadilla but Chris was a ham and cheese kind of guy.

He stripped off his suit jacket and loosened his tie before diving into the food. He'd had a busy morning and this afternoon would be dedicated to his private seminars, so he had to eat fast if he wanted to get some of the administrative tasks out of the way. After popping open the can of cola, he pushed the speaker button on his phone to listen to his voicemail.

Hi, Chris. It's Andrea. Give me or Diana a call when you get a chance, will you? Mom is acting really strange. Wait until you see her hair! She's being very secretive and won't tell us what's going on. If anyone can get something out of her, it's you. Talk later. Bye.

He jotted a note to drive over and see his mother. As the only male in the house with a single mother and two older sisters, he'd quickly learned how far charm would get him—Mom had rarely denied him anything. He'd been meaning to do some yard work for her, anyway, and that would give him a chance to find out what had Drea and Di so worried. He pushed the button for the next message.

Hi, Mr. London. My name is Amy Wong and I write for the San Francisco Inquirer. *I'd like to make arrangements for an interview—*

He erased the voicemail without bothering to hear the rest. The tabloid had been after his story for months, trying to get the inside scoop—or more likely the dirt—on the business, anything to explain the LM phenomenon. He'd never granted them an interview and he never would to protect himself and his clients from exposure.

Christopher, I'd like my mystery novels back and I have your DVDs. Let me know when it would be convenient to make the exchange. The call disconnected with an audible click.

He and Rachel had broken up after he overheard her tell a friend that he was "the guy you have sex with, not the one you stay with." When he confronted her, Rachel had accused him of investing more energy into other people's relationships rather than into his own.

She was probably right. Though he'd liked her, he hadn't loved her. In fact, he wasn't sure he'd ever really been in love. Lust, infatuation, but never love. He'd mail Rachel the books; she could keep the movies.

He played the last message. *Mr. London, this is Andrew Johnston from Hollinger/Hansen. I have good news. Our principal investor is interested in your expansion project. However, before the Board commits any venture capital, we'd like to see a more detailed business plan. Call me at 555-4642, extension 201.*

Chris dropped the last of his sandwich and played the message again. Another investment firm had turned him down two weeks ago. A wide grin spread across his face as he listened. Hot damn! It looked like he might be able to open locations in Oakland and San Jose after all.

He leaned back in his chair, lacing his fingers behind his head, and gazed through the two-way mirror at the dining room and café. He'd done it!

In high school and college, fixing up his friends had been just a game. During his years at UCLA he'd parlayed his knack for matchmaking into free meals and Bruins football tickets. Eventually he'd turned a psychology major with a minor in statistics into a flourishing business. He'd taken a gamble and made it pay off not only for himself but also for his many happy clients.

It was ironic, actually, because love had nothing to do with his success. Despite his track record for others, Chris couldn't seem to make a relationship last more than a month or so, a fact he was very careful to keep to himself. Who'd want to use a dating service run by a guy who was frequently single, a guy who didn't believe in the idea of true love he so convincingly sold?

It all came down to science, namely mathematics and chemistry. If you presented people with a potential mate who mirrored the traits they wanted to see in themselves, the probability was high that these two people would experience infatuation. After infatuation, respect and commitment would hopefully follow.

Not that he hadn't experienced a number of failures. His matchmaking skills hadn't worked at all on his parents.

Chris had been eleven when his father had dumped the family, walking out on him, his mother and sisters. He'd never seen it coming. His parents had never fought, always discussing everything quietly and rationally, and his father swore there wasn't another woman. Just some half-assed need to figure out what he wanted from life.

Chris had listened to the calmly delivered speech about things sometimes not working out the way you hope, nodding his head while his whole world imploded. He'd felt like his chest was on fire from the pressure of holding back sobs of anguish. *Don't go, Daddy. Don't leave me.* As his father turned away, the pressure bubble inside him had popped and the tears flowed freely.

It was the last time Chris ever cried.

He'd seen his father regularly, during awkward visits and strained outings, but it felt like there was a hollow space inside him. His mother had wanted her husband back, though, so Chris had done what he could—getting in trouble at school so his parents would have to meet in the principal's office. But then later his more mature attempts also met with failure...

The intercom buzzed, shaking him off that line of thought. He listened to Lara's voice. "Hi, Chris. Frank Lanvale is here for his one o'clock."

He thanked her, silently reminding himself to focus on the positive. Things were looking up business-wise. Just as long as nobody found out the truth about him or the secret of Lunch Meetings' success.

2

"YOU'RE NOT GOING out like that, are you?"

Phoebe Jayne Hollinger burst through the open door of Rei's house in Miraloma Park at exactly nine o'clock. P.J. was always prompt about her lateness. Stepping aside, Rei looked down at the white dress shirt and plain black skirt she wore with low-heeled pumps. Judging by P.J.'s incredulous tone, her best friend didn't like the outfit as much as she did.

"I think I look nice, thank you very much." Rei turned and walked toward the living room where she'd been reading in her favorite chair near the gas fire.

P.J. followed, her heels clicking on the hardwood floors. "That's the problem. You're supposed to look sexy. We're going to a nightclub, not a Bar Association function."

"I'm not good at sexy." A fact that had disappointed some of the men she'd dated. Apparently they'd expected an Asian woman to be a voracious circus acrobat in bed and a bowing doormat everywhere else.

P.J. unfastened her black satin trench coat. "You

never *let* yourself be sexy. When we were growing up, you were always afraid your father would disapprove. Later, you were too focused on school and corporate raiding—"

"That's the second time this week you've mentioned my father and I hope it's the last." Rei felt the muscles around her eyes tighten.

P.J. smirked and sank into the couch. "Don't pull the Judge Face on me. I'm immune. You know you'll have to deal with him sometime."

"Not tonight, I don't. He pushed me out of his life twenty years ago so I'm in no rush to schedule a family reunion."

Her mother had died in a car accident when she was twelve. With Keiko gone, the stately Queen Anne style house in Pacific Heights had echoed with reproving silences. Only to be interrupted by frightening drunken outbursts from a father who'd been as miserly with hugs as he had been with praise.

After two agonizing years, Gordon Davis had finally decided to move on with his life. Rei had spent all of her time with her beloved maternal grandparents in Japantown while he pursued a seat on the high court bench and a young trophy wife. Once Rei left for college, they saw each other only at the holidays.

"You're right, honey. I'm sorry. We're supposed to be celebrating." P.J. twisted on her seat and dug into the pocket of her coat. She set a small silver box on the bleached wood coffee table. "Happy Anniversary."

Rei let out a half laugh, half sob and pressed a

hand to her mouth. Her vision wavered as tears filled her eyes and a knot of emotion formed in her throat. She sat down next to her friend and reached for her hand. "Thank you for remembering, Peej. And for a lot of other reasons as well."

P.J. squeezed her fingers in return and offered a watery smile. "I'm just so glad that you're still here. There were so many days when you didn't think you'd make it this far, but I wasn't about to lose my best bud."

"God, I still can't believe it's been a whole year since the diagnosis...."

Ductal carcinoma in situ.

Her doctor had said she was lucky—lucky?—the tumor was less than one centimeter, they'd found it early, and the cancer hadn't spread to the lymph nodes. Rei's immediate reaction had been disbelief—the ultrasound tech must have screwed up because there was no history of cancer in her family. She'd been stunned and confused and sorry as hell that she hadn't gotten regular mammograms as she was supposed to.

Then she'd been terrified. She would never forget the knife jab of fear that wouldn't go away. Sure, in the abstract, everybody had to die sometime. But, not her. Not now. After that came anger, a lot of anger. At her body, at the universe, at her father who acted like it was contagious and at Jack, another of her arrogant, opinionated ex-boyfriends, who had walked out when she most needed comfort and reassurance.

After lumpectomy surgery she'd endured radiation treatment and chemotherapy sessions that had left her exhausted and nauseated. The glossy black hair she'd always been so proud of had thinned out and she'd lost fifteen pounds from lack of appetite....

Then, as suddenly as she'd been diagnosed, she'd finished with the treatments. There had been no formal exit from sick to well, just the slow physical and mental recovery until one day she woke up and the cancer wasn't the first thing on her mind. Of course, she would continue to take the Tamoxifen for another four years and have a follow-up visit every six months.

Rei had survived and in surviving had reevaluated her priorities. She'd gotten rid of a soulless renovated flat in North Beach and bought her house; taken up yoga and a healthy diet and tried to appreciate every day of the rest of her life.

Not to mention the people in it. Rei kissed P.J.'s cheek and tucked one leg up on the couch. Reaching for the box, she unwrapped it to find a silver charm bracelet. Holding it to the light revealed that each of the twelve clear crystals had a tiny pink ribbon inside.

"Oh, Peej, it's beautiful."

"A little classier than a rubber band, I thought."

Rei fastened the delicate chain around her wrist. "I love it. Thank you so much."

P.J. cleared her throat then cheerfully clapped her hands. "So, are you ready to go party with wild abandon?"

She sighed and rubbed her neck. "Actually... I had a bad day at court and I don't think I'm up to screaming to be heard over a syncopated drumbeat. Why don't we just go out for a late supper and talk?"

"Nope. You don't need talk, you need action." P.J. wiggled her brows suggestively.

Rei responded with a tiny twinge of interest. It had been awhile—a long while—since she'd had any "action." Lately there'd been an almost constant tension inside her, a restless frustration that she couldn't meditate away. Like her body was too small for the spirit within.

"We are overdue for a night on the town, but I'm not sure a nightclub is such a good idea. I've got an early day tomorrow."

P.J. crossed her arms beneath her ample bust, straining the limits of her bra top. "The whole point of this Break Away Night is to celebrate our friendship, to be a little daring and have some irresponsible fun."

That sounded so tempting. It wasn't as if she were a nun or anything. However Rei was never anything *but* responsible—to her family, to her kids at court and to herself. She had to be taken seriously in order to succeed. But maybe throwing caution to the wind was exactly what she needed. Just for tonight.

"I bought a mango."

P.J.'s forehead crinkled. "You what?"

"I bought a papaya, too."

"Oo-kay..." P.J. sat on her coat, bewilderment clouding her light eyes.

Rei felt warm spots of color on her cheeks. "I read an article in a women's magazine that suggested taking two risks a week. You know, creating a little adventure in your life. Well, I never tried those fruits before so I bought them."

"What did you think?"

She shrugged. "I liked the mango, but wasn't crazy about the papaya."

"I'll bet it felt terrific to get out of your apple-grape-banana rut."

Rei laughed. "It was oddly satisfying. Silly yet audacious. I can cross 'try exotic fruit' off of my List now."

"You're starting with the safe ones, I see." P.J.'s expression became as quiet as her voice. "How long is that list now? Wouldn't you like to shift some more items into the *Done That* column?"

The list was actually written in a bound journal her support group had given her after the lumpectomy. On the cover was a quote from Thoreau, 'Go confidently in the direction of your dreams.' Each woman in the group had received one; the idea being to create a Life List and believe those dreams could come true. Rei's book was half filled already, but with almost no check marks beside the entries.

"So, how about it, Rei? You need to cross 'dance like you don't care if anybody is watching' off the List. But not in that outfit."

And just like that she realized it wasn't only her clothes she needed to change, but also her attitude.

When she'd gotten sick, she had withdrawn into herself, organizing her life to the minutest detail. She'd thought if she could control her environment, that if she scheduled each day and always knew what she was doing, somehow she could control the rapidly dividing cells inside of her.

It was time for her to lose a little of that self-control. Over 365 days had passed since her diagnosis, six months since her doctor had declared her in remission. She deserved to celebrate. She'd earned it. Her hesitation vanished, quickly replaced by an eagerness that surprised her.

"Oh, what the hell. Let's go out and get a little wild."

With a victorious grin, P.J. grabbed her hand and pulled her off the couch. Together they went upstairs to the master bedroom and P.J. headed straight to the closet. "Take all of that off while I find something more like my outfit."

Rei looked at P.J.'s hot pink bra, sheer black blouse and hip-level skirt that barely covered her butt. "There's a fine line between 'sexy' and 'slutty' that I'd rather not cross."

"No guts, no conquests, I say."

"Hey, I just broke up with Derek yesterday." Rei unzipped her skirt and stepped out of it.

"So? It's the twenty-first century. We're not only allowed to have sex with men, but also like men."

"You mean without commitment or guilt? Do it then roll over and fall asleep?" She unbuttoned her shirt and tossed it into the laundry hamper.

P.J. turned to stare at her, obviously seeing through her sarcastic humor. "Are you telling me you've never had an orgasm?"

"I didn't say that."

"You implied it."

Rei climbed onto her bed, sitting cross-legged in her white lace bra and panties. "Okay, maybe sex hasn't been that great for me. Sometimes it was nice, but in the end it always felt like there was something missing."

"Yeah, a lover who made an effort to please you." P.J. went back to rifling the clothes hanging in the closet. "You need to add 'have amazingly fantastic sex with multiple screaming orgasms' to the List."

"It's already on there." Rei reached for the journal on the bedside table and opened it on her lap. Knowing that she'd be the only person to ever read the List, she felt free to express her secret desires.

P.J. shot her a mischievous look. "Really? In those exact words?"

"Um, no." Multiple screaming orgasm sex probably required that both partners be fantastic lovers. She didn't qualify. "Something more along the lines of 'get swept into a passionate affair.'"

"So why don't you make that the next dare?"

Rei shook her head before P.J. even finished. "I doubt that's what the magazine article had in mind."

"Oh, come on. What could be more of an adventure than acting out a sexual fantasy?"

With the men she'd dated, lawyers in a relatively

small community where her father was an Associate Justice for the Appellate Court, a part of her had held back, unable to fully give or accept pleasure. The last thing she'd needed in her bid for Commissioner was any kind of locker room talk about how she acted in bed.

But with a sexy stranger who didn't know her and therefore couldn't judge her, maybe she'd be able to let go and lose some of her self-control. With her fantasy man, she could discover and explore her sensuality. She could be a bad girl indulging in decadent pleasures.

Just the thought made Rei's pulse jump and her nerves tingle. She wanted to feel the sensual thrill of a man's hands and tongue and body touching her, stroking her, pleasing her in exactly the way she desired. To finally experience the hot, primal excitement of wild, uninhibited sex. That would be the most daring adventure of all....

Rei set the List aside. "I don't know if I could actually go through with an affair, but I'll at least be open to the possibility."

"Okay, that's a good start." With a surprised gasp, P.J. pulled a red and black outfit from the closet. "Oh, yeah. I forgot about this. This is what you should put on for tonight!"

"That was my costume three Halloweens ago, Peej." She laughed uneasily. "Judge Shuford's personal misconduct has the Ethics Committee on a witch hunt and it would be my luck to run into somebody from Court. I can't wear that."

"Sure you can. It counts as a risk for this week and, trust me, going out in this will be a lot more fun than buying fruit."

Fifteen minutes and several halfhearted protests later, Rei had changed into the red and black satin corset. It gave her small breasts the illusion of cleavage and gently nipped in her waist to create an hourglass of her slender figure. The short black satin skirt with a split over the right thigh made her legs look longer while stiletto heels added three inches to her five foot five frame.

She'd let her hair down, literally, so that the dark strands fell past her shoulders. P.J. had done some kind of makeup magic, crafting smoky shadows around her eyes and enhancing her cheeks and lips. She had to admit that maybe she could do sexy. Right now she felt daring and most definitely like a woman who indulged her inner bad girl.

Tonight, just this once, she was going to follow her impulses and see where they might lead her.

LOUD, SENSUAL MUSIC with a Latin overtone and a hard-driving bass spilled out into the night as the bouncer opened the front door to the club. Rei followed P.J. inside to pay the cover charge and get a bright red kiss stamp on the back of her hand before pressing through the crowd toward the bar. She looked around while they waited for one of the bartenders to take their orders.

The boutique Hotel Liaison was located off of

Union Square, in the heart of downtown San Francisco. The nightclub had originally been a small Victorian playhouse. The stage now served as an upper dance floor. Above it, the word *Divas* was spelled out in bright red neon with an upside-down tube of lipstick as an exclamation point.

The main dance floor occupied what had once been the orchestra pit. The balconies were used for VIP suites. Paintings of legends like Cher and Tina Turner decorated the red velvet upholstered walls and the theatre seats had been grouped around glass tables shaped like lips. Twirling spotlights and strobes illuminated the sheer yards of fabric draped from the frescoed ceiling. Even on a Thursday night, the club was packed.

"This place is awesome, isn't it?" P.J. had to lean close to her ear to be heard as she handed over a shot glass of green liquid.

Rei eyed the drink suspiciously. "What's that?"

"A melon ball shooter." She raised her glass. "To you, my friend, and living to fight another day."

"To survival." Rei tilted her head back and swallowed the sweet cocktail. P.J. smacked her glass onto the bar and signaled for another round. "Wait a minute, you're driving."

"We'll burn these off long before we leave, don't worry." P.J. indicated the gyrating bodies on the nearby dance floor.

Just then two men sidled up next to them at the bar and tried to strike up a conversation. While P.J.

seemed interested, their tired pickup lines and alpha male arrogance turned Rei off. Sure, she entertained a fantasy about sex with a stranger, but in reality she didn't want to be viewed as an easy score.

The next five or six men were no better and she got the distinct impression that this new nightclub was something of a meat market. To P.J.'s credit, she subtly accepted a couple phone numbers but stayed by her side. Finally the second round of shot glasses arrived. Rei accepted the drink, but decided it was already her last.

"What are we toasting this time?"

"To new adventures." Her friend's eyes covetously followed a hot guy walking past.

She touched her glass to P.J.'s then drained it. Almost immediately, she felt the alcohol's fire spread through her, easing the tension in muscles she hadn't realized were tight with stress. She felt light-headed, but in a good way, as if all the censuring voices in her mind had been momentarily silenced.

Rei closed her eyes, focusing on the music and chatter, the press of bodies, the faint odor of sweat and perfume. Her heart had taken on the rhythm of the music and, though the setting was incongruous for yoga, she allowed herself to be truly in the moment. Nothing mattered except being *right here, right now*.

"Let's go dance!"

Laughing at the stunned expression on P.J.'s face—usually she had to be coaxed out to the floor—she began weaving her way toward the stage. Once she reached the orchestra pit, she created a space and made room for her friend. P.J. easily got into the groove, her curvy body wriggling to the up-tempo music. Rei wasn't nearly as athletic, but quickly found her own shuffle-step-shimmy routine.

She became aware of men approaching from the sidelines and started to turn so that P.J. could shield her, then mentally shrugged. She didn't know anyone here, would probably never be in this place again. Through the mega-watt sound system, Christina Aguilera invited her to get "Dirrty." Rei gave herself over to the idea. The music was hot and so was she. Why not take a risk?

Why *not* let go and "dance like she didn't care if anyone was watching"?

"I'M GLAD YOU CAME with me, man. I can't handle all those babes by myself." Grant Bronson shoved a hand over his hair, making the already chaotic strands arch into spikes.

As they walked across the hotel lobby from the parking garage, Chris reached over to subtly knock Grant's hand down. "First off, don't think of them as 'babes.' They're people, just like us. With the same anxieties and hang-ups and goals. Come on. It's a night out at a club, not the Inquisition."

"I'm terrible at this stuff, though. I get all tongue-tied and say something stupid or make an ass of myself." He tugged at the hem of his shirt.

"Relax. There's no agenda for tonight."

Grant flinched then covered it with a grin. "I thought we came here so I can pick up babes?"

Chris held back a sigh. He'd known Grant vaguely in college, but tonight he was a client. He was a good-looking guy but it was obvious why he had trouble with relationships. He wasn't getting it that his attitude could make or break him.

"We came here to have a few drinks and meet some new people. The idea isn't to have sex, ask for a date or even get a phone number. All we want to do this first time out is assess your technique and make any necessary adjustments."

He tried to remember the last time he'd gone out for something other than work. Whether it was with a friend or a client, he seemed to spend more time giving advice than making use of it. Rachel had labeled him as only good for sex, but he hadn't been with a woman in months.

Grant's head swung around to ogle a young woman walking out of the elevator. "Wow, did you see her?"

"Yes and unfortunately she saw you, too. Put your tongue back in your face." Chris pulled up short of the nightclub's side entrance, dragging Grant over to a potted plant by the hotel concierge desk. "Listen to me. You're blowing it before you've even begun."

"What are you talking about?"

"I know it's hard to be yourself when you think 'yourself' isn't good enough. But you only get one chance to make a first impression. It's true in business and even more important in potential relationships. That is what you want, right? Because I'm not a pimp. If all you're looking for is an easy lay, you're on your own."

Grant's eyes had widened at the tersely delivered lecture, but now he looked at Chris with respect, as if he were somehow surprised. "Okay, you're right. Okay. I'm just nervous, that's all. I told you I always make an ass of myself by saying something stupid."

"In that case, rule number one is don't talk."

"Huh?"

"Women appreciate being listened to. So introduce yourself, ask about *her* then shut up and listen. Okay? Let's go." Chris walked toward the side entrance to *Divas.*

Grant caught up to match his stride. "I think it's cool that you're doing this."

"It's part of the job. No big deal," Chris offered.

"Do you give all your clients this kind of personal attention?"

"Of course. We make every effort to help people identify what makes them unique and—"

"No, I don't mean the party line. I'm talking about tonight's field trip and the clothes shopping last week. Does everybody get that or am I special somehow?"

From the minute he'd signed up for Lunch Meetings services, Grant had been full of questions, more so than most. It was starting to get on Chris's nerves…and to make him suspicious. "I can't discuss my other clients with you."

"Okay, it's cool. Let's talk about you then. Where's your other half tonight?"

Chris felt his jaw clench as he prepared to lie. "She had other plans."

Grant looked him in the eye and smiled. "Too bad. I'd love to see what kind of woman dates a date doctor."

So would a lot of other people. Chris was beginning to wonder if he should ask some good-looking friend to act as his girlfriend. Then he could stop hiding his single status and take advantage of the publicity that legitimate newspaper interviews would garner. Word of mouth would only take Lunch Meetings so far, and he really wanted to open those other locations.

They went inside and Chris led Grant to the bar where he ordered two bottles of domestic beer. The ice-cold brew was welcome, considering the heat generated by the lights and the press of bodies. He returned the smile of a woman who passed by, but made no effort to follow her. He was on the job.

Raising his voice to be heard, Chris asked Grant to point out a woman he found attractive and tell him why. Then he sent him off to try and engage her in conversation. Over the next half hour, he crashed, burned and recovered with Chris's help. Finally Grant ended up with a hot looking blonde in a pink bra and black mini-skirt, leaving him alone at the bar.

With a sense of both pride and relief, Chris ordered another beer and turned his attention to the blonde's friend. Now there was a man-eater if ever he'd seen one. The petite Asian woman was dressed to kill and her exotic appearance set her apart from the crowd, even in multi-cultural San Francisco.

Funny, though, she'd suddenly looked very lost when her friend went off with Grant....

Then the music changed, a slow seductive number that brought a delighted expression to her face. She began to move to the tempo, her hips rocking in time, while her eyes drifted shut and her lips parted to sing along. The way she danced was hypnotic and very, very arousing. She danced like she was making love.

Chris took a long pull from the beer bottle, trying to quench his sudden thirst. What he really wanted to taste was her—the golden skin, left bare by her outfit and begging to be licked. Her small but beautifully rounded breasts and that beauty mark near her mouth. Lord have mercy, just the thought of where he wanted those perfectly bowed lips left him aching.

As she dipped and turned, he admired her well-toned legs and sweet little butt. The back view was just as enticing as the front. She continued to dance, her curtain of dark hair swaying as her slim curves arched and retracted. The woman had a blatant sexuality that let him imagine how fluidly she'd move in bed. He set down his bottle and continued to watch her, not even aware he was in motion until he was halfway to the dance floor.

Unfortunately he wasn't the only male in range of her with the same idea. A guy the size of a San Francisco 49ers linebacker got to her first and tried to press himself up against her. Her dark eyes flew open and Chris had just resigned himself to several broken bones when the guy backed off on his own. He was three times her size, but she'd squared her shoulders and given him a look of cold fury before grinding her heel into his instep.

Chris couldn't hold back a smile. What a little spitfire. She tried to get back into the mood but, clearly thrown off stride by the interruption, her movements lost some of their grace. Although he remained at the edge of the dance floor, still admiring her, he made no attempt to get closer.

When another guy thought to try his chances, Chris simply thrust out an arm and shook his head. "Don't waste your time, buddy."

The other man tried to stare him down, the human equivalent of wolves preparing to fight for territory, then he shrugged and walked away. Chris allowed himself a smirk. Yeah, that's right. I saw her first. Then he realized how out of character it was. What the hell was wrong with him? Tonight was about work, not picking anyone up. He didn't consider himself a caveman type, so why was he staking claim to a woman who had yet to acknowledge his existence?

He looked back to find her watching him. Her full lips curved slightly and she nodded once before she closed her eyes again. When the song ended, replaced by a romantic ballad, she started off the dance floor. Chris figured she didn't want to be adrift in a sea of couples. He was debating whether to offer her a drink when she came directly toward him.

She looked up at him, her gaze roaming over his face, a slight flush coloring her cheeks. He got the strangest feeling she was challenging him to be worthy of her attention. Her eyes weren't as dark or as cold as he'd thought. Instead they were a warm chocolate brown fringed by long lashes and sparkling with unexpected invitation.

When she reached out to touch his forearm, his breath caught. He felt like he'd been hit by heat lightning, the kind that strikes without warning or sound. Their eyes met and sexual energy surged between them. The tingling warmth raced through his veins and straight to his groin. He stood there practically vibrating and feeling like a dork, but unwilling to break contact.

Then she slowly smiled at him, angling her head toward the dance floor. Forget what he'd told Grant about not trying to get laid. Chris returned the smile and took her hand—he would have followed her anywhere. Confidence was sexy. It was all about what you didn't say and this gorgeous woman's body language said it all. She wanted him and the feeling was oh so mutual.

3

Rei didn't need P.J.'s surreptitious thumbs up. She already felt pretty darn proud of herself.

She'd started to leave the floor when her friend walked off with a good-looking gym jockey, but the next song was one of her all-time favorites. So she'd danced by herself, letting the soft wail of the saxophone wash over her, moving her body to the beat of the percussion. She'd gotten lost in the sensuality of the music….

Only to be slammed back to reality when that arrogant Neanderthal tried to grab her. Rei used a maneuver from a self-defense class she once took then looked up to find some guy laughing at her. At least that's what she'd thought until he kept another man from approaching her. After nodding her curious thanks, she tried to get back into the song.

Although she'd closed her eyes, she still saw his wide grin and admiring expression, the disarray of his sandy hair and the casually neat dark jeans and pressed shirt. Who was this man who'd elected himself her protector? He was attractive, but there were herds of hot guys here tonight. In fact he was almost average in height with a lean build and all-American looks, and yet there was something…

And just like that she was dancing *for him.* Her whole being came alive as she imagined him watching her. Her nipples hardened beneath the satin confines of the corset and a light sweat broke out on her skin. She positioned her body deliberately, blindly enticing him with provocative gestures and sexual motions.

When the music changed, she felt drawn to him, as if he were the only man there. Maybe it was the direct gaze of his light eyes or the self-assured way he carried his trim body. Mostly she liked the way he held back, letting the decision about first contact be hers. He kept his distance even though his expression made it clear he wanted to get close, very close.

A hot flush began on her cheeks and then raced down her body to the apex of her thighs. When she touched his arm, every nerve ending jumped at the sensation. He was the one. If ever she was going to take a chance and have some irresponsible fun it was right here, right now, with this man.

He settled her into his embrace for the slow, romantic ballad. She wrapped her arms around his waist. He was so much taller that her head only came to his shoulder. Their bodies fell into rhythm with the music and with each other. Neither of them had yet to speak but words seemed unnecessary.

When two people were this strongly attracted, what really needed to be said?

His left hand rested in the center of her back while his right hand slid beneath her hair. The gentle massage made her tremble. The nape of her neck had always been an oddly erogenous spot. In response, she pressed closer to the burgeoning erection straining his jeans and felt a groan rumble up from his chest.

This kind of behavior was so unlike her. But at the same time, she was enjoying his reaction, the power of knowing she turned him on. He was a good dancer, making her wonder if he could possibly be as incredible in bed as he was on the floor. She surprised herself with the thought. She'd never been the type to engage in one-night stands yet she couldn't deny the immediacy of her desire.

Rei looked up at him then and his gaze penetrated her mind the way she wanted him to penetrate her body. A current of excitement arced between them but the next move was his. Her profession was all about being in control and taking charge. Personally, though, she wanted to be taken. She wanted to be swept off her feet and into a whirlwind of mindless passion.

Her breasts ached, the nipples tight and throbbing where they made contact with his flat belly. When she skimmed her hands down his sides toward his hips, he bent down to lower his head. She parted her lips, anxious for the taste of his mouth. But before they could kiss, the dj played a fast-tempo rap number, breaking the spell.

Her self-appointed bodyguard offered his hand again and led her from the floor. He singled out one of the bouncers, spoke quietly then guided her toward the back of the club. When she hesitated, he looked from her face to the level above the stage and back again. Several of the balconies were either dark or had the curtains drawn, offering seclusion and privacy.

So here it was, the pivotal moment. Should she take the next step, or politely decline and stay safely ensconced in reality? Looking into his pale green eyes, she saw the reflection of all her desire. She saw the answer to her question. Rei squeezed his hand in agreement and let him lead her upstairs.

His pace was unhurried as they strolled along the hallway, but the tension in his grip suggested the same urgency she felt. Eventually they found an open door and slipped inside. The balcony was decorated in the original Victorian style but Rei barely noticed before she was lifted off her feet and into his arms.

She folded her legs around his waist to keep her balance, but he easily held her so that they were face to face, revealing a strength that belied his lanky build. Below them, the music pounded from the speakers in a cacophony of sound. But up here an expectant quiet surrounded them. Even in the darkness, she could see the heat and need in his gaze and she heard it when he finally spoke.

"I don't know what I'm doing here. I lost my mind the minute I saw you." His voice was deep and slow, with the slightest hint of the South in his accent.

"You are by far the sexiest, most beautiful woman I've ever met and I want you. It's that simple."

His words frightened her, thrilled her, challenged her to give in to what she was feeling. She caressed the flexed muscles of his biceps before sliding her arms over his broad shoulders. His words stimulated her as much as the feel of his hands on her naked thighs. The throbbing between her legs became a dull ache of need that she couldn't satisfy, not yet.

"I don't even know your name."

"Chris—"

She touched her fingers to his lips, stopping him before he could give his last name. She didn't need to know, didn't want to. Tonight she was living out the fantasy of seducing a handsome stranger and it needed to remain a fantasy.

"Kiss me, Chris."

"Whatever the lady wants." He grinned, a bright and boyish smile at odds with the very grown-up feeling of his hands on her ass, then leaned in close.

His breath mingled with hers and her eyes drifted shut. She waited eagerly for the first touch of his lips and yet enjoying the prolonged anticipation. He brushed his mouth slowly, so slowly, over her lips and the sweet thrill of his touch overwhelmed her. The tip of his tongue traced her upper lip, then the lower, before slipping inside.

She returned the kiss, deepened it, faintly tasting beer and peppermint when she explored his mouth. He tightened his grip and held her against the hard ridge of his penis. Her hips began to rock in an age-old motion as she rubbed against the placket of his jeans, seeking release.

Rei moaned in protest when Chris broke off the kiss, but her moans became ones of pleasure as he trailed his lips down her neck and over her chest. He looked behind him and located a chair, then claimed her lips again. Still holding her, he sat down and spread his legs, forcing hers apart as well.

He trailed kisses along her neck as his fingers worked the top eyehooks of the corset. Rei stiffened, suddenly worried about him seeing the scar, about ruining the atmosphere with the need to explain. But then she gasped and arched her back while he suckled her left nipple.

Oh, God, what was she doing? She knew what he was doing—coaxing her to the heights of ecstasy. This was crazy. It was insane. And it felt so incredibly good.

Chris pushed her hips back toward his knees without losing contact with her mouth. She tried to scoot forward until she felt him touch her inner thigh, his fingers probing the edge of her panties. The thick tip of his thumb delved between her damp curls before circling her clitoris in a way that made her groan aloud.

Hot flames danced through her and she tilted her hips to give him better access. When he slid his thumb into her wet heat, she clenched her vaginal muscles around it and thrust her tongue deeper into his mouth to encourage him. Not that he needed any persuading. Chris both stroked and soothed, masturbating her with expert finesse to draw out the pleasure without bringing her to climax.

She wiggled on his lap, silently begging him to make her come. He withdrew his thumb and quickly replaced it with two strong, rigid fingers that worked a seductive magic on her aching flesh. He increased the pressure and the pace until he brought her to a wild shuddering climax.

Dazed, Rei slowly became aware of her surroundings, the harsh sound of their breathing and the wanton disarray of her clothing. She shook her head, trying to clear it. She'd just had an orgasm with a stranger. And a hell of an orgasm it had been. If Chris was this good at manual manipulation, actual sex with him would be phenomenal.

He seemed to have the same idea as he cupped her hips and pulled her onto his erection. His voice was husky with desire. "That was just the appetizer. Would you like to go next door to the hotel and finish what we started?"

Yes, she did. No man had ever made her feel this sexy and daring and desirable. More than anything she wanted to feel the hard length of him inside her, to give him the same level of pleasure he'd just given her. But it wasn't to be. Tonight had been an amazing experience, one to cross off the List. Tomorrow, though, she'd return to her reality.

She cradled his cheek in her hand with genuine regret. "I'll bet you make an incredible meal, Chris. But I can't."

"Don't tell me you're not still hungry." He glanced down at her hardened nipples peeking out of the corset. "I won't believe you."

Rei laughed softly and continued with the food analogy. "I'm tempted, really tempted, to order room service. I'm sure it would be delicious. But tonight was an anomaly. I don't usually indulge my appetites like this. I'm sorry."

Chris dropped his head with a groan, touching his forehead to hers. Then he sighed and didn't try to stop her when she climbed off his lap. He watched her refasten the corset with an expression of lust and disappointment. "At least tell me your name so I'll know who broke my heart."

She smiled mischievously and glanced at the bulge in his pants. "I don't think it's your heart that's giving you trouble right now."

"Okay, then tell me so I'll know who's going to be starring in my erotic dreams and keeping me awake all night."

She laughed again. This guy was smooth, definitely a player. And he wasn't being difficult, making her feel cheap or demanding his own satisfaction as she'd expected. However, to maintain the fantasy, she chose to give him a fantasy name.

"I'm Jade."

"It's been a pleasure, Jade. Hopefully one of many." He stood up and reached around for his wallet. "Here's where you can contact me the next time you get hungry."

She took the plain white card and squinted to read it in the dim light. 'Chris London. 415-555-4681.' Now she knew his last name and one of the illusions she wanted to keep vaporized. Real men with real names had real lives and reminded her that she did, too.

Rei tucked the card into her corset and arched her index finger toward the balcony door. "Are you coming?"

"Not tonight, apparently." He grinned to show he was teasing then explained, "You go on. I need a minute to, uh, calm down."

She nodded, not meeting his gaze. "Goodbye, Chris."

His soft fingers lightly grazed her cheek, as if memorizing the contours. "See you, Jade. I really hope we meet again."

She kissed him one last time, then turned and walked out, knowing they wouldn't.

PajamaPartyGirl is now online
PajamaPartyGirl is instant messaging you

PajamaPartyGirl: I cannot believe you bailed on me.

JadeBlossom: I didn't bail, P.J., I just left early.

PajamaPartyGirl: Well if you wanted to go, you didn't have to cab it, Rei. I would have driven you home.

JadeBlossom: I know you would have, but I didn't want you to have to leave just because I was.

PajamaPartyGirl: I'm sorry you didn't have a good time. You can pick the place for our next Break Away Night.

JadeBlossom: I did have a good time, honest.

PajamaPartyGirl: Uh huh. Whenever people have to tell you they're being honest, they aren't. Did that hot blond you were dancing with do something to upset you? Is that why you left early?

REI GRINNED at the computer screen. Oh, the hot blond had done something, all right, but he hadn't upset her.

If she possessed an ounce of sense, she'd be embarrassed and ashamed over making out with a stranger in a club. But the truth was, she'd enjoyed those moments of wild abandonment. Chris had joked about losing sleep but she'd been the one plagued by erotic dreams. Even after she awoke, her imagination had been running on overdrive, stirring up all kinds of sexual urges and wrecking her concentration.

JadeBlossom: No, I had a great time, the best. It just didn't work out.

PajamaPartyGirl: Oh, too bad. That explains why you seem a little short today.

JadeBlossom: I'm tired this morning and I have quite a few adoptions to approve this afternoon.

PajamaPartyGirl: Um, I forgot to remind you last night.

JadeBlossom: Of what?

PajamaPartyGirl: You said you'd come with me to look at this company I want to invest in.

JadeBlossom: Oh yeah. When is that?

PajamaPartyGirl: Monday. I set it up for your lunch hour but this place has food and I promise to feed you. Since you and Derek are over, this might work out really well.

JadeBlossom: WHAT might work out? Where are we going?

PajamaPartyGirl: To check out a dating service.

JadeBlossom: Great, Peej. Thanks.

PajamaPartyGirl: Well, it might be great for both of us. Give it a chance.

JadeBlossom: You're lucky we're best friends.

CHRIS HADN'T REALLY expected Jade to call. But he'd hoped she would. He'd lain awake most of the night, waiting for the phone to ring like some teenaged boy with his first crush. What an idiot. Finally he'd dozed off, only to dream about her. Dreams so hot that he'd ended up taking matters into his own hand, so to speak.

He loved women. He had learned from his mom and his sisters to respect women's intelligence, strength, endurance and ambition. He admired their optimism, willingness to share and their emotional depth. He had never been one to objectify women, and yet he couldn't stop imagining Jade naked.

Her body would be a perfect combination of lean muscle and soft curves. She'd smile at him as she lay back onto his bed and held out her arms. Her golden skin would be like hot silk beneath his hands. She'd gasp with pleasure when he settled between her thighs. "Chris." He could almost hear her whispering his name.

"Chris?"

He startled, realizing his next client was trying to get his attention. "Hey, Eric, sorry."

Eric Antoine slouched into the office, the picture of dejection and he flopped onto the guest chair. "I got shot down again. Why do I even bother with this? I'm never going to meet a woman who wants to spend the rest of her life with me."

"Come on, Eric. We've talked about this." He rested one hip on the edge of his desk. "If you want positive things in your life, be it love, a better job, whatever, you have to have a—"

"Positive outlook, I know, Chris. But I kept thinking about how beautiful she was and how smart, and then I got nervous because I wanted to ask her to go out with me again but I knew that she wouldn't."

He sure knew that feeling. He was dying to see Jade again but knew he'd better resign himself to never hearing from her. She would end up being a fond memory of a phenomenal night and nothing more. Too bad, but it wasn't like he was looking for a relationship anyway. On the other hand, though, his client was.

Eric was a tall, thin, African American man with big ears, a big heart and an even bigger smile when he bothered to use it. He was a nice guy with a good job but he had zero self-esteem. Chris studied his poor posture and downcast eyes.

"Is this how you talked to Michelle?"

Eric finally looked at him. "What do you mean?"

"Women are verbal communicators, men are physical. Everything about your body language right now says, 'I don't want to be here.' You can't connect with a woman if you don't make eye contact. You can't let her know you're open to a relationship if your attitude is closed. Come over here."

He grabbed Eric by the shoulder and pushed him toward the triple mirror in the corner. "Look at us. What's different?"

Eric's dark-brown eyes showed a spark of humor

as he took in Chris's paler, blonder reflection. "You mean besides the obvious?"

"Yeah, besides that." He smiled.

"You're bigger than me, and better dressed."

Chris shook his head. "I might look bigger, but I'm not. We're about the same build. Now, stand up straight. Hold your head up and put your shoulders back. See?"

In the mirror, all three of Eric appeared larger and more self-assured. His expression revealed that he saw it, too.

"Now watch this, watch what I'm doing while I'm talking to you." Chris hunched his shoulders and let his eyes shift from Eric's mouth to his hair to a point beyond his shoulder. "My lack of focus tells you what? That I don't care about you, about who you might be beneath the surface and that I'm looking to see if there's someone better to talk to."

"Ah, man. That's probably what Michelle thought, when really I was just nervous. No wonder she blew me off."

Chris clapped him on the shoulder. "Now that you know, be aware of it. If you don't get anything else out of these sessions, get this—confidence is sexy. It's all about knowing who you are inside and out. Nothing will impress a woman more."

He worked with Eric for another forty-five minutes, mostly trying to convince him that eventually he would find the right woman. Four more individual sessions with male clients followed, effectively keeping him from thinking about Jade. Sort of.

Several times, she crept into his thoughts and he had to remind himself to focus on the job. It was a lot of extra work when he could have just let the computer program handle the matchmaking. But Chris felt it was worth the time and effort.

Just because he'd never fallen in love didn't mean he couldn't make it happen for someone else.

Not long after he opened Lunch Meetings, Chris had realized that too many of his early applicants just wanted to get in, get off and get out. Even those men who wanted to fall in love were more likely to screw up a budding relationship than the female clients. Either they made mistakes at the beginning or they weren't willing to put in the effort to keep it going and they walked out when things got too complicated.

Like his father.

So Chris began quietly offering courtship counseling to the men who seemed genuinely interested but totally clueless. Using his own experiences and education, he helped his clients reform their self-image and destructive behaviors. Sure, it was manipulative. But it worked and that's what mattered.

At least it worked for other people. He'd seen it happen, helped make it happen, but in that hollow void inside him he didn't believe it would happen for him. He was much better at fixing other people's lives than finding lasting happiness in his own.

THE AFTERNOON DOCKET cleared quickly and the day ended on a high note, as Rei approved the adoption of a seventeen-year-old girl. A special hearing had been set so that Katie could be a legal member of the Kaufmans before she aged out of the system. After granting the petition, Rei had her picture taken with the tearfully happy Kaufman clan—Katie, two big-hearted parents and their six other adopted children.

Rei was still smiling as she packed her belongings for the weekend. At least until she remembered that she was going home to an empty house. Something that usually didn't bother her. But, focusing on the briefcase full of files and petitions, suddenly the old caution about all work and no play came to mind.

Rei walked out of the courthouse and down into the parking garage. The idea of playing naturally segued into thoughts of Chris. She hadn't allowed thoughts of him to distract her on the bench, but he'd definitely been on her mind all day long.

And each time she recalled the image of his handsome face and roguish grin, her heart beat a little faster. Her nipples got a little harder. Her thighs got a little damper. Despite the explicitness of what they'd shared last night, she shouldn't care who he spent time with. But she couldn't help wondering what he was doing tonight.

And with whom...

As she slid into the driver's seat of her Lexus, she heard a faint buzzing noise from her handbag. Reaching into her purse, she pulled out her cell phone to answer the call. "Hello?"

"Rei. It's Maggie Solís."

Her heart clenched in her chest. Something about the oncologist's compassionate tone of voice had her gripping the phone tighter, anxiety building inside her like layers of fog on the Bay. "Dr. Solís. What—? I mean everything was fine when I left your office."

"I know, Rei, I'm sorry. You've been asymptomatic and I only ordered the blood work as part of your routine exam. But I got the results back from the lab today and… I'm sorry."

Rei's pulse fluttered erratically and her hands began to shake as she listened to the medical jargon about glycoprotein markers. Apprehension swirled in her gut, making her voice quaver when she was finally able to speak. "Are you sure?"

"No, not for certain. That's why I'd like you to have a mammogram and MRI first thing Monday morning. Just call my secretary and let her know when you're done so we can expedite the findings."

Hot tears streamed down her cheeks as Rei dully agreed and thanked Dr. Solís for her concern. But as the phone dropped from her numb fingers into her lap, raw grief assailed her. She lifted a trembling hand to her mouth, inhaling deeply through her nose, hoping not to throw up, fighting the urge to scream.

It couldn't be true. This couldn't be happening again.

The same sharp-edged fear she'd experienced last time came back with a vengeance. It wasn't fair.

Survivor was supposed to mean that the ordeal was finished, behind you, over. With the cancer in remission for over a year, she was supposed to be making plans and looking forward to the future....

4

"REI, HAVE YOU BEEN crying?" Candace Versa laid a hand on her arm and frowned in concern.

After leaving the courthouse, Rei had driven over to California Pacific Medical Center to meet her breast cancer support group. She didn't know how she would have endured her last bout with the disease if not for P.J., Dr. Versa and these brave women.

She'd originally planned to come this evening to share her one-year triumph with the women who best understood. Instead, she would cast a specter of gloom over a group that tried their best to hold on to the light. If there were any people on the face of the earth she could share her situation with, it was the women in this hospital conference room.

The educated uncertainty made it worse this time, knowing as she did what was at stake and what would have to be done. Tears pierced the back of her eyes again. But Rei held back, not wanting to confront this new turn of events yet. She didn't want to put her dread and fears into words and make them real.

So she forced a smile of reassurance onto her lips. "I'm fine, Candy. I just had a bad day at work."

"Well, you know I'm here if you need to talk."

"I know. Thanks. I'm okay, though."

Dr. Versa patted her arm again before Rei slipped past her to take a seat among the others. There was a core unit, including Dr. Versa, a psychologist, as well as with other women who joined and left over time. Rei greeted her old friends and nodded a welcome at the new faces as everyone introduced themselves.

"Hi, Kerry Kensington, two years." The petite redhead always brightened the meeting whenever she attended.

The quiet brunette next to her was new to the group. "I'm Heather Centrino, and um, it will be six months next week."

"Alicia Rexam, I'm a three-year survivor." Despite her silver white hair, she didn't look old enough to have seven grandchildren.

"I'm Rei Davis and it's been…one year."

And so they went around the room. As they were finishing the introductions, the door opened behind her. Rei turned to see who had joined them and gasped softly at the sight of her friend Miriam.

"Sorry I'm late, ladies." Miriam's voice was breathy and she slowly made her way to the table.

Rei's heart broke as she watched her friend gingerly lower herself into the chair. They had been born the same year, but now Miriam looked at least a decade older. There was a tightness around her mouth, as if she were in a great deal of pain, and her skin had a grayish pallor. Her brown eyes were dull and held a shadow of fear even as Miriam looked at her and winked.

Cold certainty crept over Rei. She may or may not be sick again, but there could be no doubt that Miriam was.

"It's good to see you." Dr. Versa smiled at her in welcome. "We were just about to share List accomplishments."

Rei was frankly dreading this part of the meeting. She couldn't tell them about her sexual encounter with a stranger in a nightclub. She'd have to settle for relaying her exotic fruit experiment, an accomplishment that sounded lame compared to Alicia finishing another quilt for her grandchildren or Kerry learning to ice skate.

"If you don't mind—" Miriam paused, closing her eyes briefly with an audible pant. "If you don't mind, Candy, I'd like to say goodbye first."

Rei's heart skipped, anticipating hearing the worst. *No, not Miriam.*

"I want to thank you all. For the camaraderie and tears, laughter and hugs. I can't imagine how I would have gotten through this. Without my friends." The sudden appearance of tears washed the dullness from her gaze. "But I won't be coming back to the group."

Murmurs of sadness and comfort echoed throughout the room.

"Honey, no."

"Oh, Miriam."

"Don't, don't feel sorry for me, girls." She panted again, her smile now a little frayed around the edges. "Howard and I have been preparing for months. We're finally taking our dream trip. France and Spain for as long as we can afford to stay."

Rei laughed out loud to relieve some of the tension that had built in her chest. "You're really going? That's wonderful!"

The noise level in the room rose with excited chatter as Miriam gave details about her upcoming trip and the rest of the group shared the experiences they had recently checked off of their Life Lists. Rei listened absently to the conversation, lost in her own thoughts.

Miriam might be dying but she was also fully living at last. Her attitude and daring silently reminded Rei of how fortunate she'd been last time. Despite her depression and doubt that she might not be so lucky this time, she didn't dare wallow in self-pity. Not when her friend was fighting so bravely.

Across the table, Miriam gave a breathy laugh in response to something Alicia said and Rei realized how much she would miss her. Her friend had always tried to look on the positive side, telling off-color jokes to make everyone laugh and baking a cake in tribute to each month of survival.

The best way for Rei to honor her friend's legacy of courage would be to follow her example. Like

Miriam with her trip to Europe, she needed to celebrate the good things in life and not wait for dreams to come true, but to make them happen. Starting right now.

HIS SISTER WAS RIGHT. There was definitely something strange about his mother.

Jeanna London had always been a constant in Chris's life. She'd had the same job at the same accounting firm for years, lived at the same house in Lower Piedmont where he'd grown up, kept the same general routine. Like the air, she was just there and didn't require much thinking about.

So when he walked through the bright blue front door of her white stucco house after work, what he saw took his breath away.

"Mom?"

He'd expected to find her curled up on the couch, wrapped in her favorite sweatpants and cardigan, watching the evening news. Instead, she was transferring her wallet and stuff into a little beaded purse. Her light-brown hair was streaked with golden blond highlights and cut to shoulder length. Her shoulders were bare except for the straps of a figure-hugging black dress.

He didn't even know she had a figure.

"Mom?"

"Hi, sweetheart. This is a surprise." She walked over to where he'd stopped dead in the hallway and air-kissed his cheek, careful not to smudge her dark pink lipstick.

"Not as surprised as I am." Chris couldn't get over how…how sexy his mother looked. Moms weren't supposed to look that way! "What did you do?"

She glanced at the foyer mirror and smiled a little even as she took him to task. "Aren't you the one who teaches men how to pay a compliment? You're not exactly bowling me over here."

He gave her a real kiss on the temple. "Sorry, Mom. You look fantastic."

"That's better." She went back to emptying her everyday handbag.

Chris stuffed his hands in his pockets and leaned against the stair rail. "What prompted the haircut and… Everything? Is there some charity benefit for work tonight?"

Her smile widened but she didn't answer as she straightened her hem and fluffed her hair. The sort of last minute primping a woman does before going out on a date.

Chris's chest tightened painfully at the thought. Over the years, his mom had gone to dinner with male colleagues or out with a group of friends, but she hadn't dated. The pressure in his chest increased and he realized he was holding his breath, a stress-related habit. He flared his nostrils and forced air into his lungs, hoping he was jumping to conclusions.

"I came by to finish that yard work, but it's all been done. You didn't lift those heavy bags of mulch yourself, did you?"

"No, I didn't." She moved to the hall closet then held a heavy black wool cloak toward him.

Chris frowned but helped her into her coat. "So, the Henderson kid came over?"

"No, he didn't do it." She grabbed the evening bag and her car keys from the hall console.

"Come on, Mom. What's going on?"

When she turned to look at him, he saw the stubborn set of her jaw but also a bright gleam in her eyes. "I'll tell you when I'm ready."

"Obviously you're going out tonight and that's great. I just want to know what you're doing."

The hint of tension in her posture belied the casual tone of her words. "I have a date, Christopher."

Here he was an adult, yet all these years, neither of his parents had shown an interest in anyone else. All these years, he'd childishly wished they would somehow get back together.

Don't think about it. Don't let it hurt.

He forced his jaw to unclench and tried to match her nonchalance. "Give me the guy's name so I can check him out."

"I already know he's a good man."

Chris took her elbow as she opened the front door. "For Pete's sake, Mom, you can't know for sure—"

"Trust me." She gently pulled out of his grasp. "I appreciate your concern, but you'll just have to trust me." She turned and stepped outside, walking down the three stairs while he closed the door.

What the hell was with all the secrecy? She'd

always let him into her life. After his father left, he'd been the man of the house, making it his responsibility to be strong for his mother and older sisters. He'd thought he and his mom were close but all of a sudden she was shutting him out. Was this new man that damned important to her?

He allowed a little of his anger to color his words. "At least tell me where you're going tonight so I'll have a last location to give the police."

"I'll be fine. There's no need to call out the Marines."

He didn't share her joke. "Just because I'm out of the Corps doesn't mean I've forgotten my combat training. Where is he taking you?"

His mother just smiled wider and unlocked her car. "I love you, tough guy. I'm going to Palio d'Asti, okay?"

"Hunh. Somebody wants to make a good impression."

She looked at him then, her gaze suddenly as serious as her tone. "Yes, I really think he does. People change, sweetheart. Remember that."

The new Jeanna London gave him a quick hug before sliding into the driver's seat. Chris stood in the driveway and watched her pull away, a frown tugging at his mouth. A band of tension reminded him he was holding his breath again and needed to lighten up.

As he walked back to his Dodge Dakota pickup truck, he reflected on the irony of the situation. His love life sucked. Here it was Friday night and the successful dating service owner was going home alone while *his mom* had a date.

SLOWLY FLIPPING the pages of her Life List, Rei reviewed some of the dreams, goals and aspirations she'd written over the past months.

Visit New York City during the holidays
Drink wine in an olive grove in Tuscany
See the Aurora Borealis
Drive a Mazerati
Swim with the dolphins
Try either hang gliding or skydiving
Snorkel on the Great Barrier Reef

Rei closed the book and flopped back against the bed pillows. Before she'd been diagnosed last year, career ambitions and fear of failure had kept her in a uncomfortable space, leaving her wary of stepping outside of her chosen box. Once the disease had gone into remission, though, she'd planned to embark on all kinds of great adventures.

But somehow, over too short a period of time, she'd slipped back into a similar box—this one just included a different job and more interesting fruit. Now, it was very possible that she was getting sick again and this time it could be terminal. Honestly, she didn't want to know. Not yet.

Avoidance was a cowardly way to deal with the likelihood, but would a few days or even a week really make that much difference?

They might, if she put the time to good use. She vowed to adopt singer Tim McGraw's lyrics about living like she was dying as her personal anthem. She would likely have to face another round of treatment soon enough. Before then, though, she wanted to cross as many things off her List as she could.

She now realized that she had followed the letter of the support group assignment, but not the spirit. Did goals have any real meaning if you never took steps toward achieving them?

She needed to stop daydreaming about out of the ordinary adventures—there was no way she could take off from work to hike the Grand Canyon or go whale watching in Alaska right now. Instead she would take the kind of small personal chances that added richness and depth to each day. Trying new varieties of fruit might not be life altering, but it had been fulfilling.

And then, whenever she could, she'd let go of her fears and excuses in order to take some bigger risks, like she had at the club last night. Seducing a stranger had actually been a pretty big item on her List. But had she really fulfilled her objective? She definitely didn't feel fulfilled.

She got up from the bed, suddenly too restless to sit still, too aware of the mattress beneath her. Tossing the Life List on the comforter, she went to the window. She rested her forehead against the glass, looking over at the lights from the streets downtown. The cold against her temple did nothing to alleviate the heat coursing through her.

It was crazy to want a man so much, to imagine having sex with a virtual stranger. Crazy because, for all she knew, Chris was out there right now seducing some other woman in some other nightclub. It was stupid to think the sparks she'd felt had been mutual, that last night had been anything special. She'd better write the experience off as a once-in-a-lifetime fantasy partially accomplished and forget about him.

Except that forgetting him proved impossible.

Each time she closed her eyes, she experienced again the heat of his touch and the drugging taste of his kiss. She remembered how he'd made her feel, how quickly he'd taken her over the edge. She wanted to feel that way again without the barrier of clothing between them. She imagined having hot, primal, sweaty, earth-shakingly satisfying sex....

If she stepped outside her sensual cage, there would be no going back. Her safe little world would be irrevocably altered. And she wanted it to be. Rei lifted the phone and forced herself to dial before she lost her nerve. Right now she didn't care if this was crazy.

Because, no matter what logic her mind tried to enforce, her body knew exactly what it wanted. And what could be more life affirming than making love?

CHRIS REACHED INSIDE the doorway of his loft in Oakland and flipped the switch. Simulated daylight filled every corner from one end of the 850-foot space to the other. He hated the early evening gloom of mid spring, the way the rains swept in from the Pacific as evening overtook the city.

The singer who'd left his heart in San Francisco had probably never spent April here.

Chris laid the pepperoni and bacon pizza on the breakfast bar as he passed the open kitchen and headed for his office to drop his briefcase. His oldest sister, Andrea, was an interior decorator. She liked to use his condo as a testing ground for new ideas and the result was a different design style in each section of his home. Right now his office area looked like the inside of a ship, all done in gleaming teak and brass.

And it was occupied.

"Hey, how'd you get in here?"

The fourteen-year-old boy sitting at his computer firing arrows and spells at the Uruk-hai advancing on Helm's Deep didn't take his eyes off the computer screen. "Hi, Uncle Chris. I, uh, caught a couple of Muni buses then walked the rest of the way."

He arched his brow at the incomplete answer. "How'd you get into my apartment, smart guy?"

Gabriel finally looked at him, both pride and anxiety in his deep brown eyes. "I talked my way past the doorman with a sob story and then used an extra key."

Chris decided not to bother asking when or how he'd gotten a key made. "Do your parents know where you are?"

With a sullen expression, Gabe turned back to the video game. "Like they care."

"I'll take that as a no." He reached for the phone on the desk.

"Aw, come on, Uncle Chris—"

He spoke quietly, but firmly, in his best I'm-the-adult voice. "They need to know you're okay."

"Whatever."

"I'll let you share my pizza while you're waiting for somebody to pick you up."

"Whatever." Gabe seemed to be concentrating on the game, but then he slid Chris a sideways glance as his stomach rumbled. "What kind of pizza?"

He reached down to tousle the kid's dark-blond hair as his sister answered her cell phone. "Hi, Diana. How are you?"

"Busy. I just finished showing three houses and now I have to get across the city for a settlement. Is this important?"

Chris ignored the agitation in her voice. "I'm fine. Thanks for asking. Gabriel's fine, too."

"Gabriel?"

"Yeah, you know. Your son?"

The boy muttered darkly, the words too soft for him to make out, but things were blowing up all over the computer screen.

Diana didn't have a sense of humor at the best of times, and right now he could hear her cursing the slow moving drivers around her. "I know who he is. What about him?"

"He's here at my place." The silence that followed told him that Di hadn't even realized Gabe was missing. "I'm calling because I figured you'd be worried."

"Thanks, Chris. Damn it, watch the road! Look, I'm sorry, but I don't have time to come across the bridge to get him. Can you call Michael? I've got to go."

Gabriel avoided his eye as Chris set the phone down but the tension emanating from him was palpable. Suppressing a sigh and a whole lot of things he'd like to say about his sister, Chris dialed Mike's number. He got a similar "I've got other things to do" attitude from his brother-in-law, who was still at the office, and so offered to drive Gabe home himself.

Chris laid his hand on the boy's shoulder, feeling the tight muscles beneath the Bay Academy school T-shirt and hurting for him without knowing how to make it better. "Why don't you shut down the game and we'll go eat."

He led Gabe back to the kitchen, a large open space that resembled a particular Italian chain restaurant. It had a brick oven he'd never used, a forty-eight-inch programmable six-burner gas stove he didn't know how to use and an empty deep freezer that he only used for bags of ice when he threw a party.

Chris grabbed a couple beers from the French door refrigerator—root beer for Gabe and a real one for himself—then joined his nephew at the breakfast bar. Forgoing plates, they ate the pizza straight out of the box. He killed time on idle small talk about work and classes, waiting until they were on their third slices before asking about the unexpected visit.

"So, G-man, what's going on?" The answer he got was a shrug. "Something must have prompted you to spend ninety minutes on public transportation to get over here."

Gabe seemed fascinated by the strips of bacon on his pizza. "I called Nana, but she said she was going out."

Chris grimaced. "Yeah, she's got a date."

"Get out! Who's the dude?" His brow wrinkled in disbelief.

Not wanting to admit he didn't know, Chris turned back to the topic at hand. "Guys aren't usually big on talking about their feelings, but the rules are different when beer and pizza are involved."

Gabe dropped his fifth slice back into the box, apparently not hungry anymore. His narrow frame seemed to shrink as he slumped in his chair and fought to control his expression. His voice quavered when he finally spoke.

"Mom and Dad are never home these days. When they are, they're fighting. About money, their jobs and stuff, about me getting in trouble at school. I'm worried, I mean, I think they're serious this time. They keep yelling about a divorce."

Damn. It seemed Michael and Diana had been building towards this for a while. Chris wished he could say he was surprised, but none of the three London kids had done well in their relationships. Neither his parents nor Gabe's seemed to realize how deeply their decisions left invisible scars.

He reached over to wrap an arm around Gabe's shoulders. "I'm sorry, kiddo. I don't know what to say. But I'll tell you this much—been there, done that and lived to tell the tale."

Gabe leaned toward him, accepting the comfort for a brief moment, before shrugging off Chris's arm and moving away. "Got anything for dessert?"

A half gallon of chocolate almond vanilla ice cream later, Chris sat near Gabe on the couch, not really watching TV so much as just being there. When Mike called to say he was home, Chris drove Gabe back to Richmond in a silence that intensified the closer they got to the house.

"I know you don't believe this, G-man. But, whatever happens, you're going to be okay."

"I guess."

On impulse, Chris grabbed his nephew around the neck and planted a kiss on his forehead before Gabe got out of the truck and walked up to the door.

NINE O'CLOCK and he had the long stretch of a night alone ahead of him.

As he got closer to home, Chris drummed his fingers on the steering wheel, his eyes on the road visible in his headlights but his mind on his empty condo. It was late to get together with friends and he wasn't in the mood to sit at a bar or go to a club....

Inevitably his thoughts turned to Jade, the exotic temptress with the sultry eyes, the memory of whose sinuous movements and incredible sensuality had dominated his daydreams. Dreams of holding her on his lap while she rubbed against him, moaning in that breathy way of hers.

He reached down and adjusted his aching erection. What was wrong with him? It wasn't as if he'd never been with a beautiful, sexy woman before. He'd dated some real lookers, slept with some total knockouts. But none of them had affected him like Jade. He wanted to kiss her again. For about a week. Then he wanted to strip her bare and kiss every inch of her delectable little body. Then he wanted more, much more....

The quick chirp of his cell phone interrupted his fantasy. The ringing continued as he lowered the window to let the cool air blow against his face. He picked up the phone and flipped it open, his voice raspy as he answered.

"Um, hi, Chris. This is—Jade."

"Jade?" His brain took a few seconds to process the reality of hearing her voice.

"Yes, from Divas!"

Wow. Fantasies came true? The next thing he knew, cash would rain from the sky and his pickup truck would transform into a vintage Corvette. His face split into a wide smile, but he tried to keep his voice casual.

"How could I forget? This is just kind of a surprise."

"Is it?" Her tone implied the call had been inevitable. And as he remembered the electric instant they first touched, maybe it had been.

What should he say? Something about the previous evening? Something about being unable to forget her? Something about being glad she called? Something about wanting her so badly it hurt? Whatever he said, it had to be smooth.

"So... How are you?"

There was a brief hesitation before he heard her take a breath. "Last night you said that what we'd shared was just an appetizer. Well, tonight I'm hungry, Chris. Very hungry."

5

HE GOT A speeding ticket. He didn't care.

Chris had turned the truck around and made it from one end of the city to the other in just under twenty minutes. Chris careened into the parking garage of the Fieldcrest Hotel, tossed his keys to the valet, jogged toward the elevator then turned back for his parking stub, before taking the stairs two at a time to reach the lobby.

Once there, he took a minute to catch his breath. Jeez, you'd think he'd never been on a date before. He wanted Jade under him, over him, any and every way he could have her. But she didn't have to know all that the second they met again. Chris walked across the marble tiled lobby to the Hearthstone Pub. His gaze immediately picked her out of the crowd.

She sat at the bar, her hair upswept and her ankles crossed. But there was nothing prim about the way she looked. Metallic threads in the gold sweater she wore caught the low light. The deep cut neckline teased him with a hint of cleavage and her black silk pants flowed along her legs like water.

Amid the noise and hum of voices, Jade seemed utterly prepossessed, sitting patiently on the bar stool and ignoring everyone around her. Chris walked up and brushed a hand along her shoulder, both in greeting and for the pure pleasure of touching her. She didn't even startle, as if it never occurred to her that anyone else might touch her.

Jade looked up at him and smiled. "Hi, again."

"Hello yourself. Can I buy you a drink?"

She considered it for a second then nodded. "Sure."

Chris looked at the bartender. "A draft beer for me and the lady will have…?"

"Maybe a shot of tequila, I think."

He chuckled at the contradiction of her decisive tone and uncertain words. "Really? I would have guessed you were a white wine drinker."

Jade gave him an enigmatic smile. "I'm trying new things."

"All right. Then go for the best. Two shots of Cuervo 1800 Gold, please, and a glass of ice water."

They sat in a surprisingly comfortable silence, not touching and yet hyper-aware of each other. Chris was perceptive to the heat from her body, the scent of her skin and the hint of uncertainty in her eyes even though she kept them averted. She glanced at her hands then around the bar, looking everywhere except at him. Jade seemed less confident than she'd been at their first encounter and he wondered what had happened.

Practicing what he preached to his clients, Chris

set out to put her at ease. "I'm glad you called. I haven't been able to stop thinking about you."

She finally looked up and the heat of her gaze seared him. "You've been on my mind as well. Last night was…hard to forget."

He laughed, having noticed where her eyes had focused.

The bartender set two small glasses, a shallow dish of salt and a bowl of limes in front of them. Chris paid the tab then stopped Jade from reaching for a lime wedge. "This is premium quality tequila, aged to be much smoother. So we don't need the taste killers."

"If you say so." She tipped her head, lifted her glass and touched the rim to his.

Watching her with veiled amusement, he knocked back the shot and began silently counting. One, two… He didn't wait long. Jade's eyes widened then started to tear as she dropped her shot glass on the bar top and gasped for breath. He handed over the ice water and grinned.

After several sips, the bright color in her cheeks receded and she was able to talk. "Smooth, huh?"

"I spent a wild drinking weekend in Tijuana back in college. Trust me, this is smooth." Chris shook his head when the bartender gestured for another round, thinking she'd probably opt for a different drink next time. "Do you still want to try something new?"

Jade dropped her gaze again, a slight frown between her brows, and didn't answer. She toyed with her shot glass, rotating it between her palms one way and then the other. Her expression fascinated him. Despite her sexual confidence and provocative outfit, her long dark lashes couldn't shield her insecurity.

It would seem that the exotic temptress had an unexpected conservative side.

Chris stroked his fingers along her arm before offering her an out. "You said on the phone you were hungry. We could have a light dinner at the place across the lobby." He angled his head in the direction of Shrewsbury's. "Or would you rather go somewhere else?"

Just when he figured they'd be going to the restaurant, she raised her head and he watched her draw a deep breath. She looked right into him and in her gaze he saw both hesitation and longing; caution and white hot desire.

Whoa. Apparently he'd misinterpreted her expression. Jade was definitely a bad girl trying hard to be good—and failing.

"I'd rather go upstairs."

His stomach clenched, as did other parts of his body, but he didn't let his reaction show. He just nodded slowly, playing it cool. "Okay—"

"But first we need to talk."

Chris reached out to take her hand. Her fingers were warm within his grasp and once again he felt sparks of attraction travel along his nerves. "I'm not seeing anyone right now but, when I was, I was careful."

"Thanks for answering what I couldn't ask." Jade

smiled at him and relaxed a little. "But the other thing we need to talk about is what you expect of...this?"

He knew better than to put up boundaries at this early stage, thereby limiting what could be. This was exactly what he cautioned his clients against. Hadn't he recently chastised Grant about only wanting to get laid? But since she was being honest, he would be, too.

"I recently ended a relationship and I'm not looking to get into another one."

The rest of the tension in her shoulders released along with her breath. "Great. And since there's obviously a strong attraction between us, I thought maybe..."

"Maybe we could have some fun, just enjoy each other?"

She laid her other hand on his thigh. "And you're okay with that, right?"

"More than okay. I told you last night I wanted you and I've only wanted you more in the past twenty-odd hours."

"I want you, too, Chris. More than I expected. But what I don't want are any...complications. Can you handle the idea of just mutual satisfaction, no promise of anything more?"

He allowed a slow grin to spread over his face. "Are you propositioning me, Jade?"

She raised their joined hands and brushed her dark pink lips across the back of his, all the while holding his gaze. "Absolutely."

He leaned forward on his bar stool and cupped her cheek in his palm. He brushed his mouth over hers until she parted her lips and returned the kiss. He explored her mouth slowly, thoroughly seducing her in public without getting them arrested. Finally, he moved back.

"I'll go and see if there are any rooms—"

Jade stopped him with the lightest touch on his arm. "I took the liberty of making a reservation after we hung up earlier."

He grinned at her forthright expression. "You figured I was a sure thing, huh?"

"I'd hoped you might be."

Chris stood up and held out his hand. "You were right."

SHE WAS ABOUT to have a one-night stand.

The elevator doors slid shut without a sound and yet Rei heard a definite slam in her mind. Was she really going to have sex with a man she'd just met and still didn't really know? This went beyond dirty dancing and fondling in dark corners. Slowly, the elevator began its ascent, moving her inexorably toward the point of no return.

The electronic room card burned in her hand. Of course Chris would be a gentleman about it if she said she'd changed her mind. When she glanced up at him, he was already looking at her. He didn't speak or touch her, but simply held her gaze in the same quietly passionate way he had at the club. Then he slowly smiled.

Seeing it should have paralyzed her with self-doubt. Oddly though his smile had the opposite effect. In that instant, her insecurity vanished. She wanted this, she wanted him, and gladly threw out the imaginary key that would keep her real persona locked away. She chose "Jade" over "Rei" tonight. Jade the confident seductress. The bad girl.

Acting on pure impulse, she turned and threw herself into his arms. When he bent down and pulled her closer, she traced the edge of his lip with her tongue before sliding inside to explore his mouth. The tequila tasted better on his lips than in the glass.

Her hands fisted in the soft material of his shirt as she deepened the kiss. He pulled the clip from her hair, allowing it to tumble down her back before threading his fingers through the long strands. Holding the back of her head, he thrust his tongue in and out of her mouth. It was a blatant promise of things to come.

Slanting her mouth over his, she tugged his shirt out of the waistband of his jeans then slid one hand beneath the cotton fabric. Her fingers brushed over the light dusting of hair on his belly. He groaned against her lips when her hand grazed his left nipple and it beaded in response.

Cupping his hands over her butt, he held her against his rock hard erection, leaving no doubt as to how much he wanted her. Her entire body came alive and the rush of pleasure almost brought her to her knees. Not a bad idea, actually.

Omigod! Had she actually just contemplated…? Rei broke the kiss, her breath ragged. "How much further?"

Chris chuckled softly. "All the way, just as soon as we get to the room."

"Until then, go stand over there." She pushed him with a lighthearted shove.

He did as she asked, crossing his arms and resting his back against the wall, but his green eyes glowed with mischief. She felt his stare practically burning holes in her clothing as he swept his gaze up and down her body. The look was thrilling and not without challenge.

Chris grinned and dropped one hand to the waist-band of his jeans. He held her gaze then looked down as he leisurely slid his hand lower. She followed the movement then caught her breath. Her eyes widened at the sight of his large hand cupping his zipper even as her belly clenched in pure lust.

But two could play that game. Rei's usual pre-sex anxiety had been stifled by the bravado of her new persona. Feeling bold, she parted her mouth and deliberately traced her index finger across her lower lip. Watching his expression, she glided her fingers along her chest and beneath the edge of her sweater to circle the side of her breast. Her nipple hardened at the touch and as she watched his lips part, she longed to feel his mouth on her flesh.

His eyes darkened and her pulse fluttered in primal recognition. She tensed, awaiting the moment when he claimed her and suddenly liking the idea of going at it right on the carpet. If she was going to be daring, she might as well find out how far she could go. Chris seemed to have the same idea. He'd just pushed away from the wall when the elevator dinged. They had reached their floor.

"Saved by the bell, lady."

The sigh that escaped her was more frustration than relief. "I thought it signaled the beginning of the first round."

Chris laughed and took her hand as they counted room numbers along the corridor. "The first one, huh? Your confidence will either inspire me or kill me."

"Don't worry." She slid him a flirtatious glance. "I know how to give mouth-to-mouth resuscitation."

"Want to test your skills, just to make sure?"

Chris tugged her to a stop in front of their room, wrapping his arms around her shoulders. His lips pressed down on hers then his tongue slipped between them. She kissed him deeply, desperately, wordlessly expressing how much she wanted him.

Her whole body was throbbing when she finally managed to shove the electronic card in the slot and open the door. Chris stumbled inside with her, his mouth still sealed to hers, then lifted her against the wall and held her there while they kissed some more. Oh man.

The need for him was so great she trembled as she pushed at his shoulders and gasped for breath. He set her down and backed away, stripping off his jacket as he moved into the room. Rei followed, tossing her coat and purse into the closet and kicking off her shoes.

By the time they stood together in the center of the room, she had stepped out of her satin pants and he was barefoot as well as gloriously bare-chested. The faint golden light from the doorway illuminated the ridges of muscle along his torso as he held out his arms.

In the time it took for her heart to beat, she was back in Chris's embrace. Giving in to a tactile impulse, she stroked both across his broad chest then up over his wide shoulders. Hot velvet skin stretched over hard lean muscle, the kind that spoke of active fitness instead of a gym membership.

He devoured her lips. His kiss was hungry, deliberate and thorough. Rei melted against him, letting him take whatever he wanted. She wanted him to be in control, to make her experience sex like she'd never had before and love every second of it.

Her hands slid around to the smooth skin of his lower back while his roamed underneath her sweater to fondle her left breast. She'd never been happier that her small size had allowed her to go braless. The difference in their heights hindered them, though, so without breaking contact, Chris guided them toward the end of the bed.

He fell back so that she landed on top of him and Rei wriggled up his big body to capture his lips again. She thrust her tongue deeper into his mouth while his hands groped her bottom and thighs. The hard bulge of his erection pressed against her hip and she moaned at the thought of having him inside of her.

He tugged her sweater over her head and cast it aside to expose her breasts. Lifting his head, he took her sensitive flesh into the heat of his mouth and sending a bolt of desire through her body. Rei braced her arms on the bed and gasped, her breathing as quick as her heartbeat.

His right hand slid under the edge of her panties and between her legs, making her moan aloud. Damp heat flooded his fingers as he wiggled them inside of her. Then his thumb circled her clitoris as he'd done before, setting off a series of clenching ripples that had her straining for release.

When his hand stilled, it took a second to realize she wasn't going to get what she needed. Dazed with lust, Rei smothered a groan of frustration. "What's wrong?"

In the faint light, his expression looked sheepish. "Uh, we need to stop. In my rush to get here, I didn't have a chance to take care of things."

He wanted to stop? What for...? Oh.

"It's okay. I have protection in my purse."

Chris grinned at her. "You really did think I was a sure thing, didn't you?"

She shrugged while returning his smile. "I was feeling unusually confident when I called you, so..."

"So, hurry up and get that condom."

Rei rolled off the bed and scrambled for her handbag. Within seconds, she'd returned to the bed and tossed several strips of foil packages onto the comforter. Chris looked at her, then at the dozen condoms and back at her.

"Your confidence is going to kill me for sure."

She laughed lightly at the irony. Actually confidence—a lack of fear and a sense of daring—was going to save her. "What a way to go, huh?"

Rei hooked her panties with her thumbs and yanked them down her hips. She tossed them over her shoulder and flopped onto the bed while Chris shed his trousers and underwear. She heard a tearing sound as he opened a condom wrapper. Then he was beside her again, the heat of his large body raising her already soaring temperature.

He nuzzled his mouth over her right breast, alternating wet kisses and greedy suckles, as he positioned himself between her legs. The hard length of his rigid penis prodded her most tender flesh. She shivered in response, in anticipation and need. But just when she thought—hell, she hoped—he would pin her to the bed and ravish her, she felt him tense.

"Sorry. I shouldn't have been so rough."

His mouth had been near the crescent-shaped scar on the underside of her breast. Now she tensed as well, the sexual mood in danger of breaking. Damn it, she didn't want to have to explain and suffer his pity. "I don't want you to be sorry. I want…" To be treated like she was normal and healthy.

"What, Jade?"

Hearing the name was all it took to give her the

courage to say something she'd never dared to before. "I want hard, fast, furious, mind blowing sex."

Even in the dim light she saw the bright gleam of his smile. "Whatever the lady wants."

All rational thought vanished in the haze of lust along with any insecurity or self-consciousness. Rei opened herself to him, hooking her ankle over his calf and giving him freer access to her center. The tension in the muscles of his arms and back were her only warning before he pushed himself into her tight, wet passage.

She gasped, arching her hips as her body adjusted to his thickness and length…. And then he moved. Oh how he moved, plunging and withdrawing at a deliberate pace set to slowly drive her crazy.

When he levered himself onto his elbows, she raised her head to watch. It was incredibly erotic to both see and feel his thick shaft as their bodies joined and separated. He pulled back, inch by inch, then slowly squeezed forward again, making her shudder with the fulfillment of it.

She let her mind shut down and instead listened to her body telling her what it needed. And right now it, she, needed everything that Chris was doing to her. Again she experienced the first wondrous aching in her belly. Chris must have felt it also because he quickened his pace, increasing the glorious grinding pleasure.

Wrapping her legs tightly around his thighs, her hands clutched at the sweat slick muscles of his back.

She barely recognized her own voice. "More, Chris. I want more."

He didn't need her encouragement. Slipping his hands beneath her hips, Chris drove into her, each stroke stimulating her more than the last. Feeling wild and wanton, she reveled in the hard, fast thrusts. She'd never felt so out of control and she loved the freedom of it. Her body was on fire, her vaginal muscles clenching around his pulsating shaft.

He filled her again and again as she writhed beneath him, urging him on with breathless moans and restless hands. The pleasure became so intense that her climax was all but ripped out of her. He pistoned his hips, driving heavily into her heat. Her body clenched around him as a guttural moan ripped from his throat, and he exploded inside her.

Breathing hard, Chris dropped his head to the mattress but carefully supported his weight on his arms. Rei lay beneath him with her eyes closed, her body languid but her mind racing. Wow, the saying was true, she never knew sex could be like that. When she'd decided to seduce a stranger, she hadn't anticipated how it would make her feel.

Desirable, powerful and, oh, so sexy. With Chris, she'd been able to ask for and get exactly what she wanted, without a single worry about what he thought of her. In fact it had been incredibly liberating to let him take her while she simply let herself enjoy the experience.

But she'd felt something else as well, an unexpected connection. Why had this man been able to satisfy her, more than satisfy her, in ways that none of her past lovers ever had? Why did she feel as though she could relax and trust him when logic deemed it entirely too soon?

And what happened now? It would be a mistake to let down her guard, to allow this encounter to be anything but physical. She had no idea what she would be facing in the coming weeks. But she knew from past experience that she couldn't expect him to stick around.

CHRIS DIDN'T usually indulge in casual sex, but he might just have to change his mind on the subject. Something about Jade's asking for "fast, furious and mindless" had freed his more primal urges. He'd wanted not only to protect and pleasure, but also to dominate and impress.

Beside him, she whispered softly, "Wow, I never knew it could be like that."

He grinned at the ceiling. She sounded pretty impressed. He turned his head to press a kiss to her temple. "A lot depends on the chemistry you have with your partner."

"I guess I've never had the right partner before."

She leaned over to trace the edges of his mouth with her tongue. He parted his lips, inviting her to go deeper, but she seemed content to slide her mouth slowly across his. He gently nibbled on her plump lower lip until finally she thrust her tongue forward and explored his mouth.

She shifted on top of him, brushing her soft lips over his neck, making him quake as desire burned along his nerve endings. The universe narrowed to the places where their bodies made contact. He felt the heat of her skin against his, the rasp of her pebbled nipples on his chest and the rough silk of her pubic hair brushing his belly.

There was no way he was ready, not yet anyway. But, oh man, the way she was wiggling felt good. He'd just have to slow her down so he could recover and then—she'd moved down to take his left nipple into her hot mouth. The wet tugging sensation sent a bolt of lust right to his groin.

Her tongue blazed a hot, wet trail from his chest, along his abdomen and down to his groin. She eased lower, nipping his belly, licking his thigh and finally darting her tongue over his cock. He dragged in a breath, gasping at the shock of that wickedly intimate kiss.

"So, Chris, when do we start round two?"

He was fully erect and more than aroused. He closed his eyes briefly, lost in the sensations her touch elicited. Then he felt her mouth gently sucking the tender flesh in the crease of his hips and discovered a new erogenous zone.

"Right now."

He pulled her roughly into his embrace and claimed her mouth, kissing her long and hard, a kiss she returned with equal enthusiasm. Pressing his body to hers, he rubbed one thigh in between her legs, stroking her. He breathed in the musky scent of her desire as he felt the dewy soft folds of her labia against his skin.

Already he was rock hard. He hadn't thought it was possible so soon after the last time. Reaching out blindly, he grabbed another condom off the strip without losing contact with her lush mouth. As soon as he'd protected them, Jade got to her knees and swung one leg over to straddle him.

A slow ragged sigh escaped her throat as she sank down onto his rigid shaft. Flexing his hips, he slipped easily inside, burying himself to the hilt. He thrust into her, slowly, deliberately. She rocked her pelvis back and forth to increase the friction until he couldn't distinguish his moans from hers.

Then, arching her back, Jade braced both hands on his thighs, changing the angle of penetration. He grunted as the new position increased the pressure on his cock and intensified the pleasure. She tossed her head back and laughed, but her laughter quickly turned into squeals when he pressed his thumb to her clitoris.

The erotic massage to her most sensitive core sent her into a frenzy. Chris lay beneath her, sweat drenched and grinning while she rode him like a thoroughbred at Bay Meadows racetrack. He felt the change inside her, felt her body tighten around his shaft, and he increased the pace.

She continued to ride him and he rode the storm of mind-blowing sensations as she came hard, and then came again. Pushing deeper, pumping harder, he called out a moment later and shuddered over the edge of his own release.

His heart thundered in his chest and he lay beneath Jade's glistening body, gasping for breath. Her skin smelled of flowers and satisfaction. Exhausted and spent, Chris wrapped one arm around her waist and gently rolling her off him. Tucking a pillow under her head, he kissed Jade's love-swollen mouth then dragged the comforter over them.

Yep. There was definitely something to be said for finding the right partner.

HE MUST HAVE drifted off because he awoke to hear the jangle of a key ring. Chris opened his eyes. A quick glance over his shoulder revealed the sun was barely approaching the horizon. Then he turned over to see Rei fully dressed and pulling on her coat.

So, this was it. Whatever they had started was already ending. It shouldn't have bothered him.

"You're leaving?"

His sleep-roughened voice seemed to startle her. Poised beneath the entryway light, he saw the resolve in her expression. "Yeah, I am. Why don't you get some more sleep? Check out isn't until eleven o'clock."

"Why don't you come back to bed and not sleep at all?" He tried to keep it light but his chest tightened at the thought of her walking out. "Were you even going to say goodbye?"

She dropped her gaze and at least had the decency to look embarrassed. "I have to… I've got to go."

Pushing the covers aside, he swung his legs off the bed. "If you'll hang on a minute, I'll get my clothes and buy you an early breakfast."

"Thanks, but no." She moved closer to the door.

As he approached her, he saw her eyes roam over his naked body and seized on the attraction between them. "Listen, I know this was probably supposed to be a one-time deal. But it doesn't have to be."

She shook her head before he'd even finished the offer. "We agreed, Chris. So I don't think we should plan on dating."

"No, not dating. More like…seeing each other." He kept his hands at his sides with an effort. He wanted to touch her, to connect somehow, but didn't think she'd welcome it. "We don't have to make any promises, just be open to the possibilities and in the meantime have some good, safe fun."

The corners of her mouth lifted in an odd smile. "What makes you think this is safe?"

"The lack of illusion and the absence of commitment. We can simply enjoy each others' company, explore our desires and take our time deciding about the rest."

He caught the sudden anguish in her expression before Jade reached for the handle and turned away. "Thank you for a wonderful night. I'll never forget it."

Chris grabbed the edge of the door, careful to keep his naked body out of view. "Wait, I don't have your number. How—"

"I'll call you." She threw a quick smile over her shoulder and slipped through the opening.

"Jade—"

Chris raked both hands through his hair and sighed. She was gone.

6

Sunday, April 13th

> Accomplishments to Date: Eat dessert for break-
> fast; Go to Alcatraz Island; Visit Yerba Buena
> Gardens; Walk across the Golden Gate Bridge

"THIS HAS BEEN a pretty great weekend." P.J. bit into one of the Vietnamese lobster and prawn spring rolls and moaned.

Rei speared a pan-grilled scallop from the bed of endive and watercress. "Yes, it really has."

They were having a light Sunday supper by the infinity pool in the Nob Hill Spa. Rei had treated them both to a day of *longevity, serenity and tranquility* services. The soothing rhythms of Spanish guitars seemed to drift out of the water. She smiled content- edly and gazed out the window at the spectacular colors over the cityscape from Huntington Park to the Bay.

"So what's going on with you, Rei?"

She looked away from the sunset to find P.J. eyeing her shrewdly. "Nothing's going on. I'm just enjoying the view."

"I'm your best friend, honey. Don't bother lying to me." P.J. set down her fork. "You act relaxed after all the prodding and pummeling today. But, from your expression, you still seem like you're on edge."

She should have known Peej would notice her mood. And she'd pegged it correctly, too. Rei felt liked she'd been both caged and set free by Dr. Solís's call.

A part of her wanted to share the burden she was carrying, but the other part intended to keep her fears to herself. As stupid as it sounded, Rei didn't want her to worry. Especially since P.J. would mercilessly harangue her into the doctor's office and she just didn't want to face that yet.

"It's nothing, Peej. I just have a couple of things on my mind that's all."

"You're thinking about your anniversary, aren't you?" P.J.'s blue gaze softened. "You're finally taking that List of yours seriously. Is that why you dragged me out to play tourist yesterday?"

Rei shrugged casually and chose one of the glazed plantains from her plate. "I've lived here all my life but had never visited those places before. Since you hadn't, either…"

"Uh huh. As afraid of heights as you are, I still can't believe you didn't throw up when we got to the middle of the bridge. Why would you force yourself to go across if something wasn't going on with you?" A slight frown appeared between her golden brows.

"Stop borrowing trouble, P.J. I just like your company and your friendship, okay?"

"Okay." But P.J. still looked skeptical, with lines of concern bracketing her eyes, as she started eating again.

CHRIS MADE a conscious effort not to scowl at his client. It wasn't Marvin Carrington's fault he was in such a bad mood. Oh sure, the weekend had started off great. What could be better than meeting the woman of your fantasies and then having that sexual fantasy come true? But he'd crashed back to reality much faster than he'd expected.

How the hell could she just walk off into the night after that? He regarded himself a pretty good lover, considerate and giving. He'd tried to make his time with Jade memorable and, for him at least, it had been the best sex of his life. The whole seduction had affected him more than he'd planned.

Okay. Maybe he was blowing things out of proportion and all it had been was just sex. But, damn it, he'd felt…something.

Stunned and rejected and oddly hurt. Yeah, he knew he had no right to feel used. He and Jade had agreed up front about what they wanted and the terms had been clear. But that didn't stop him wanting to see her again. It didn't stop him from checking every now and then that his cell phone batteries were charged—

He startled, realizing his client had been trying to get his attention. "Sorry, Mr. Carrington. What was your question?"

"I was asking about the match profile. Do I have to put up a picture right away?"

Chris looked at the nice but chubby, balding chiropractor and smiled reassuringly. "No, not if you don't want to. You can wait until you connect with someone."

How long did that take anyway? Was he mentally exaggerating the bond he felt toward Jade?

"Great." Mr. Carrington's shoulders slumped, as if he didn't believe it would happen either. "That will give me time to find a professional photo studio."

"Don't do that, Marvin. Just choose a picture from your family album. That's the best way to let people get to know the real you."

He scoffed. "The real me? The real me hasn't been on a date in almost a year."

"There is somebody for everybody, Marvin. The key to finding that person is being yourself. Remember, you're a great guy with a lot to offer a woman."

"Thanks." He nodded gratefully then continued reading the brochures.

Chris made a mental note to follow up if Marvin decided to use the service—he might benefit from a little coaching. Hell, he could use a little coaching himself right now. How was he supposed to forget a woman whose image had etched itself onto his brain?

He leaned back in his chair and glanced through the two-way mirror. Lara, the office manager, was at the entrance shaking hands with a tall blond woman. The prospective client was a real looker, and even the light gray business suit she wore couldn't hide that fact that she was built like a centerfold.

A woman like that needed a dating service? Then again, every guy from the mailman to the mayor probably hit on her. It was possible she wanted to find a man who appreciated more than her looks. He turned his attention to the short brunette Lara was greeting now. There was something familiar about her....

She was dressed in a dark blue pantsuit, her hair tightly wound into one of those complicated French styles. When she turned, he saw that she was Asian. She wore wired-rimmed glasses and an impatient expression. Her face looked bare except for pale lipstick—Chris jerked upright—and a beauty mark.

"Are you okay?" Marvin asked.

"Uh, yeah. I'm fine." With an effort, he tore his eyes away from the window. Marvin gave him a quizzical look. "Did you have any other questions?"

"Actually, I was wondering how the e-mail thing works. Do I have to come here every time I want to check it?"

That couldn't possibly be Jade. Could it? How did she find him. His card only had his name and cell phone number. Focus on Marvin. Focus. "Oh, um, remote access. The e-mail is set up as an intranet, but you can access it remotely through a secure section of the Lunch Meetings Web site."

Marvin picked up the next brochure and Chris swung his head back to the window fast enough to give himself whiplash. Lara was leading the two women to her office. Now he'd get a good look when they passed by.

"What about the billing schedule, Chris. How—"

"Hang on a second, Marvin."

Lara and the blonde were engaged in conversation, but the brunette glanced at the mirror as she walked past. The plain white shirt and dark jacket couldn't camouflage her innate sensuality. The glasses couldn't obscure the liquid chocolate gleam in her big brown eyes. And nothing in the world could hide that luscious come-and-taste-me-baby mouth.

That was his Jade, all right. And damned if she was going to need a dating service.

AFTER LARA VOIGT explained how to activate the computer program and took their lunch orders, she left them alone in one of the café's partitioned cubicles. Rei clicked on the "create profile" button to begin the compatibility process. The first screen asked for contact and credit card information.

P.J. reached into her purse. "Hang on, let me get my American Express. This was my idea, so I'll pay for it."

"We just sat through the whole presentation. Why do I have to go to the trouble of setting up a profile?"

"The owner wants to open two other locations. The Board of Directors has dismissed me as a clueless Paris Hilton clone. So in order to convince them to let me invest in Lunch Meetings, I have to show them how well the service works."

"I still don't understand why the Board's opinion matters. Your father left Hollinger/Hansen to *you*."

"Daddy left me controlling interest, with the stipulation that I have to consider his cronies' advice on all decisions. These guys are a tough sell. That's why I need you to go through the entire process."

Rei studied her friend's innocent expression. "You're full of it, Peej. You're just trying to set me up again."

"That, too. I'll get a firsthand—or rather second-hand—look at how the business operates and you'll get to meet some new guys."

She rolled her eyes before quickly typing in her name, address, cell phone number and P.J.'s card number. The next screen came up for her to fill out a general description—a checklist on a scale of one through five, five being the most true, one being the least.

"Section one of seven? How long is this going to take?"

"Not long if we do it together." P.J. pulled her chair closer. "Click five for *clever, introverted, perfectionist* and *quarrelsome*. Only click three for *content, humorous, patient* and *communicative*. And, let's see, put ones for *lazy, arrogant, under-achieving, optimistic* and *passionate*."

Rei disagreed with the passionate part. Surreptitiously touching the jacket pocket where she'd tucked his card, she thought about Chris. About the gleam of desire in his eyes and delicious softness of his mouth. About that naughty little thrill he'd somehow known about. She thought of the incredible night they'd spent together and the memory made her thighs clench against a ripple of wanting.

She'd hoped for good sex and gotten better than she'd imagined. Her pulse beat a little faster as she recalled the way his hands felt on her body and how he felt inside her. Remembering the expression of utter bliss on his handsome face, Rei felt proud of herself, knowing she'd made him as crazy as he'd driven her.

Was Chris really such a good lover, or was it because of her own change in attitude? Maybe their coupling had been so good because there was no emotional investment, no strings or complications. Because she didn't feel the need to impress him or to worry what he would think of her after having sex "on the first date," the sex had been the best she'd ever had.

When she'd told Chris she would call, it had been an empty promise, a kiss off to smoothly end the awkward parting. But twice today she'd almost dialed his number. Now that her inner bad girl had been unleashed, it seemed that side of her didn't wanted to be shut away anymore.

"I'm checking a four on that last question."

P.J. looked at her. "I know you're doing me a favor, but this isn't going to work if you're not honest about your answers."

Honesty changed with circumstance, though. Rei wouldn't have considered herself passionate before.

Chris had awakened that side of her. Who would look at the conservative Commissioner Davis and guess what "Jade" had done Friday night?

"I can be passionate, damn it."

"Put a five next to *stubborn*."

Lara came back to their cubicle ten minutes later, bringing chicken salads and glasses of iced tea. "How's it going, Rei?"

"I'm only on section three. There are a ton of questions and they aren't all that easy."

"Successful relationships take work." Lara smiled before turning to leave. "Don't forget to create a user name and password for your e-mail account."

"What do you think, Peej? Should I use my real name?" Rei took a bite of her salad.

"That's up to you, but personally I'd use initials or a nickname. Even with the background check, you never know who might be contacting you."

"Okay, then. Um, how about RLD49?"

P.J. smirked. "You and your football."

"I know it's been a decade since the 49ers made the Super Bowl, but they have a great lineup this season. Their time is coming, trust me." Rei set up her new e-mail and moved on to the next set of questions.

The *Personal Characteristics* section asked her to rank things like, "I feel guilty if I am not being productive" and "I have a high level of desire for sexual activity." The *Important Qualities* part asked her to indicate the traits she sought in a partner. The *Vital*

Attributes questions required her to check off her values, beliefs and relationship skills.

Thirty minutes later, Rei finished the extensive set of questionnaires and hit the "save" button to send her profile to the database.

P.J. smiled at her with a combination of mischief and sincerity. "Here's hoping you find the love of your life."

CHRIS CLOSED THE DOOR to his office, barely able to keep from slamming it. Marvin's application process had taken longer than planned so he'd missed any chance of confronting Jade before she and her friend had left.

He'd had to casually ask Lara about the appointment to find out which of the women had applied. Now that he had Rei Davis's name, he could read her profile summary and maybe figure out why she'd given him a false identity.

Since his computer had the main server access as well as monitoring override ability, he was able to immediately pull up her file. He noticed that she'd left her occupation blank. Also the mailing address and billing address were different.

What was she trying to hide?

If it were anything criminal, the background check should find it. Beyond that, he'd have to investigate on his own, a prospect he eagerly looked forward to. Jade's name might be a fake, however the attraction between them had been real.... Real hot. She sure hadn't hidden her desires or her passion, not that first night in the bar nor the night they'd gone to bed.

His throat suddenly felt tight and his face was getting hot. He knew it was ridiculous to feel jealous—he only just met her—but he hated the idea of anyone else being with her, touching her the way he had. The way he wanted to again and again and again.

On a whim, Chris started the compatibility search engine to see which of his clients the computer thought she should be paired with. The search would take a few minutes, so he got up and went to the credenza for a glass of water.

The computer beeped to indicate it had finished matching the traits and attributes of the hundreds of profiles in the system. Chris went back to his desk to see which men the program had chosen. He did a double take when he saw the list on his screen, then stifled a chuckle.

He had forgotten that the tech who'd written the programming script had needed a sample profile to work from. According to the carefully coded, regularly tested and virus scanned proprietary software program, Chris and Jade—or rather, Rei Davis—were 99% compatible.

Almost a perfect match.

MONDAY AFTERNOON, Rei took the bench five minutes behind schedule.

"Is everything all right, Commissioner?" The

court service clerk spoke softly as Rei hurried into the courtroom, still fastening her robe.

"It's fine, Mary Alice." Rei smiled briefly. "I had a lunch meeting."

She took a deep breath as she pulled her chair under the bench. It wasn't like her to be late. Or flustered. But that's how she felt about signing up for the dating service. A part of her considered it nothing more than a silly favor for a friend. A part of her dismissed it as embarrassing and desperate.

Yet another part quietly wondered if maybe she'd already met someone. Someone charming and sexy and quietly assertive. A man who made her feel desirable and daring, a man who made her scream with multiple orgasms… Rei looked up to find everyone in the courtroom staring at her. She felt the heat between her legs travel all the way to her face but waved a hand to indicate she was okay.

"Let's get started. I see Mr. Dowd and I know Mr. Bates had a family emergency. Ms. Green, I assume you're here for Bruce Grayson?"

Shambala Green, a regal African American woman, stood up, placing a hand on the boy's shoulder. "Yes, Your Honor. Jeff Bates asked me to take over under the circumstances. I'm sorry for the delay of this morning's hearing."

"Please extend my sympathies to Mr. Bates when you next hear from him." Rei fanned the papers in front of her, looking for a particular report. "I've read over the Grayson file, including the police, hospital and psychologist's reports. I'm ready to hear arguments. Mr. Dowd?"

"Thank you, Your Honor. First off…"

Rei let the Assistant State's Attorney's words drift over her while she watched Bruce Grayson's face. Unlike the swaggering petulance he'd exhibited last week, this afternoon he looked like what he really was—a vulnerable child at the mercy of the juvenile justice system.

"Excuse me, Mr. Dowd. I'd like to hear from Mr. Grayson."

The ASA stuttered to a halt at her interruption. "Ms. Green is welcome to present her case after—"

"Sit, Mr. Dowd."

Rei turned her attention to the twelve-year-old hanging his head at the defense table. "Mr. Grayson, do you have anything to say to this court?"

The boy lifted his head and looked over his shoulder at the empty gallery. Even at a distance, Rei could see his eyes water. He turned back around, once again hanging his head, and remained silent.

She tapped her fingers on the arm of her chair. "Mr. Grayson? Bruce. You have to know the gravity of the situation. I am in the position of deciding the fate of your life for the next several years. Have you nothing to say?"

Bruce sighed deeply, his round face tightening as though he fought strong emotions. His words came out as a broken whisper. "I just… It wasn't supposed to— I had to do it so Brandon would see…. I'm so sorry."

Rei's heart twisted as the boy began to cry in earnest, finally expressing remorse for what he'd done. With prompting from Ms. Green, Bruce haltingly explained that his older brother, Brandon, was a member of the Westmob gang. Bruce thought that if he passed the gang initiation, he could live with his only remaining family instead of in foster care.

When Bruce finished, Frank Dowd stood up. "Your Honor, no matter what his motivations, the fact remains that Mr. Patterson has several cracked ribs and a skull fracture. The brutal nature of the assault precipitated a heart attack. Bruce Grayson's deliberate, and now it would seem premeditated, act cannot go unpunished."

"And it won't, Mr. Dowd. But what I'm seeing here is the act of a child, a misguided and confused child. My ruling is that Bruce Grayson stand trial here in Family Court, with a sentencing recommendation that he receive psychiatric counseling during his time with the California Youth Authority. Mr. Grayson, I strongly suggest you take this opportunity to redeem yourself, to turn your life around and make something positive of it. We're adjourned."

Bruce Grayson stared at her in grateful disbelief then nodded his head. For one brief and shining moment, he smiled at her before the bailiff led him out. Rei sincerely hoped Bruce would make the most of the second chance she'd given him and that she'd never see him before her bench again.

Monday, April 14th

> Accomplishments: Try sunrise Tai Chi in the
> park; Sign up for French cooking class; Write
> a fan letter to favorite author

REI WAS WHIPPING up a cheese and mushroom omelet
for supper when the phone rang. The caller ID
flashed P.J.'s number as she picked up the handset.

"Will you represent me if I get arrested for
popping one of Dad's friends in the mouth?"

Rei took the sautéing mushrooms off the heat.
"Bad day at the office, Peej?"

"This guy all but patted me on the head." P.J.'s
voice raised an outraged octave. "He said that since
I'm so interested in this dating service, it must
finally be a sign that I'm ready to settle down,
implying of course that I should be barefoot and in
the kitchen."

Rei glanced down at her naked feet but decided
against mentioning them.

P.J. was still talking anyway. "So have you heard
anything yet? Have hundreds of hot guys begged you
to go out with them?"

Rei rolled her eyes and began whisking milk into
the bowl of eggs. "We just signed up this afternoon.
I seriously doubt I'll hear from anyone this week."

"You'll let me know, though, right?" P.J.'s tone
had turned unusually anxious.

"This really means a lot to you, doesn't it? I

mean, more than just wanting to make an investment in a promising business."

There was a pause and then she heard a heavy sigh. "Yeah, this is important, Rei. It's about proving myself. I know you understand that."

Kent Hollinger had been dead for over five years, but his ghost and the stipulations in his will still haunted P.J. She was smart enough to control the reins of the finance company—she just needed the chance.

"Yeah, sweetie, I do. I'll check the e-mail right after dinner, okay?"

Hello, Rei

Welcome to Lunch Meetings. Thank you again for signing up for our services. We hope that this will be a rewarding experience and look forward to helping you find the person you're searching for. You currently have "4" new messages in your inbox. To access them, go to www.lunchmeetings.net and log in with your user name and password. This is a secure server and you can be assured that each message has been virus-scanned.

Good luck and don't hesitate to contact us if you have any questions.

The staff at Lunch Meetings

Four messages already? Rei was impressed and not a little intrigued. She connected to the Internet using the computer in the spare bedroom. If the service got match results this quickly, it was no wonder the business was doing well and P.J. would be smart to invest.

Hi, RLD49
The system said that we're compatible and I couldn't wait to introduce myself.
I already have a high level position in waste management and a close relationship with my family. Now I'm looking for a woman who's open to a traditional long-term commitment.
Please answer this e-mail soon.
DumpsterKing1

Rei made a face at the monitor as she deleted the message. It sounded like the King was pretty desperate. She'd dated a guy like him once. "Close relationship with family" likely meant he lived with his mother. "Looking for a traditional long-term commitment" probably meant he was anxious to marry someone else who would cook for him and do his laundry.

She opened the next e-mail, this one from Shy-GuyinSF.

Hello,
My name is Carter. This is my first time using a dating service. From your profile, you seem like a nice person.
Would you like to have lunch sometime? If so, just let me know when. I look forward to meeting you.

Carter didn't seem that shy to her. In fact, she admired the simple honesty of his message and the courage it took to make contact with a stranger. However, she wasn't about to lead him on by having lunch with him, not when she didn't really want to get involved. She mentally wished him well as she deleted that message, too.

The next message was more like a form letter, using the exact wording from the list of introductory icebreakers that Lunch Meetings had provided.

Hello, RLD49

In order to get to know each other, I'd like to ask you the following questions:

1) Describe some personal habits that are important to you.

2) During a typical week, what physical activities do you enjoy?

3) What do you like to do on your day off?

And to show my willingness to be open, I'll share my answers:

1) It's important to me that a woman be clean shaven and that she doesn't swear.

2) I'm not really into exercise, but I do have a treadmill in the basement

3) I like to go bird watching or visit a museum.

I can't wait to read your answers and I hope we can have lunch soon.

SD1975

It would be a long wait. SD1975 seemed creepier than DumpsterKing1. Why ask about physical activity if he didn't do any? Besides, she wasn't sure whether clean shaven referred to her chin or points south. Maybe P.J. shouldn't invest after all. With a sigh, Rei opened the last e-mail.

TO: RLD49
FROM: DCL3
HI THERE
I hope you had a good day. Mine was pretty great—I got some news at work.
Listen, I know the computer says we're compatible, but maybe we should judge that for ourselves? If it's okay with you, I'd like us to get to know each other a little via e-mail first.
What do you think?

Rei smiled at the computer screen, relieved that DCL3 seemed normal. His message conveyed an easy-going charm, as if they were already old friends just touching base at the start of the week. She shouldn't answer him though, for the same reasons she didn't reply to Carter. Why waste everyone's time if she wasn't looking for a relationship?

She read the message again. Then again, if she were going to help P.J. with her decision, maybe she ought to find out more. She could always break things off as soon as they went too far. She composed a quick reply, in what she hoped was the same friendly tone, and clicked "send."

7

"So, uh, how's everything going, son? You doing okay?"

"Yeah, Dad. I'm fine. How about you?"

Chris wrinkled his brow in confusion. David had called him out of the blue, apparently to chat. His father never chatted. When they spoke it was always a brief, stilted conversation about a specific topic like asking for help with a home improvement project or what to get Gabriel for his birthday.

"I'm good, I'm good. Uh, how's business?"

"Lunch Meetings is doing great, thanks. So, what's up?"

David cleared his throat. "I haven't seen you in awhile. I thought maybe we could get together. Maybe meet at that sports bar you like."

His brows arched toward his forehead. His father was not a big sports fan, nor was he one to hang out in bars. But now his curiosity was aroused. "Sure, Dad. How about Thursday night for happy hour?"

"Sounds good. So, uh, okay then. I'll see you there."

Chris hung up the phone and decided that both of

his parents were acting weird. He wondered if his father had somehow found out that Jeanna was dating again. The idea of permanently losing her to another man may have prompted a need to get closer to his kids. He'd check with his sisters later to see if David had called them, too.

Opening the notebook computer on his desk, Chris moved the mouse around to click on the e-mail icon. His Lunch Meetings account forwarded copies of messages to his private address. When the program opened, his eyes skimmed down the sender line until he spotted the reply he'd hoped for. With a grin, he opened the message from RLD49.

RE: HI YOURSELF
I think that's the best idea for now. I'm very big on judging things for myself, so not meeting right away is fine with me.
My day was pretty good, too. I think I may have made a difference in someone's life. Always a good feeling.
RLD49

Chris frowned slightly at her reply. He hadn't said anything about not meeting. But if she was new to Internet dating he guessed he couldn't blame her for being cautious. He'd follow her lead and just play it cool, though that's the last thing he felt when he thought about her.

RE: THE DIFFERENCE
It's a great feeling, isn't it? My clients have told me that what I do has changed their lives, too.
So, I have a really exciting night planned. Cold beer, hot chicken wings and a sci-fi movie marathon on cable.
How about you?
DCL3

RE: PARTY CENTRAL
My night is going to be *much* more exciting than yours. I'm going to the gym, then, because I'll probably need it, I plan on taking a hot bath with a good book.
RLD49

Chris stared, unseeing, at the e-mail. He was picturing Rei in that bathtub, without the book or anything else to obstruct his view. She would close her eyes and rub soapy lather over her bare breasts, then down the length of her body and between her thighs. The hot water and her arousal would bring a pink hue to her golden skin....

His fingers flew over the keyboard, composing an intimate reply, and then froze. He couldn't say any of that. Rei didn't know that he knew about Jade. Chris tapped the backspace button and deleted the text, not sure what to say but knowing there was no way he could voice his lust and frustration.

RE: ENJOY
I hope you have a good night and I'll talk to you later.
DCL3

He closed the e-mail program. He didn't know whether Rei would write again, and if she did, would she be more open with him electronically than she had been in person. He also didn't know if "Jade" would call again, nor whether she'd let him get to know more about her than which physical touches made her moan his name.

Feeling like he didn't know anything anymore, Chris got up to grab a beer and watch that movie marathon.

Tuesday, April 15th

Accomplishments: Try kickboxing; Eat junk food all day; Volunteer to be a literacy tutor at the library

REI'S STOMACH rumbled as she approached the restaurant on the first floor of the courthouse building. It had turned out to be another short cause day with a heavy caseload. So the chance to have lunch with her friend and fellow Commissioner, Sarah Whitney, was a welcome break.

Running into Associate Justice Gordon Davis was not.

Her father was leaving Indigo at the same time she and Sarah arrived. He was as good-looking in his sixties as he'd ever been, a combination of wise statesman and gracefully aging actor. His silver-shot hair swept back dramatically from his forehead to emphasize his piercing brown eyes.

Eyes that at the moment regarded her with the expression of faint disapproval she'd never understood.

"Hi, Dad."

"Hello, Rei."

He glanced around, as though some of his peers might be watching, then grasped her shoulders to hold her six inches away while she kissed the air near the cheek he turned.

Perhaps sensing the tension, Sarah touched her arm. "I'll go in and get us a table."

Rei nodded absently, then spoke to the young man standing beside her father. "Hi, Hunter. How's it going?"

"Good, really good." Her eighteen-year-old half brother gave her the same awkward kind of shoulder squeeze her father had. "How about you?"

There was no sense in being honest since her "family" rarely saw each other except on holidays. "I'm fine, thanks."

"Hunter, tell Rei your news." Gordon didn't wait for his compliance, instead making the announcement himself. "He's been accepted to Stanford. And, of course, he'll go on to Stanford Law when he finishes his undergraduate work."

The look he cut to her was an abbreviation of the indictment she'd endured when she had chosen Boalt

Hall instead of Gordon's alma mater. UC Berkeley's school of law was also ranked among the nation's top ten, but that hadn't mattered. Now, at last, her father had a true heir, a son molded in his own image.

"Congratulations, Hunter."

"Yeah, well, as I keep getting reminded, Stanford is a big deal. Not only did Dad go there, but so did Supremes Rehnquist and Day-O'Connor."

She wondered whether it had really been Hunter's choice at all and felt sorry for the boy with whom she shared blood but no kind of relationship. "You'll be in good company."

Gordon smiled at the fair-haired young man. "I'm proud of you, Son."

Rei had learned at a young age to clamp down on any feeling regarding her father, but somehow the insidious hurt seeped around the edges. She looked over at Gordon, who had glanced toward her at the same time. For a moment their eyes, so alike and yet belonging to such different people, met and held.

She hoped her expression didn't reveal all the longing and resentment squeezing her throat closed against unasked questions. *Are you proud of* me, *Dad? You've never said so. Do you love me? Did you ever?* But she held her tongue as always.

Gordon broke contact first, looking at the gold watch on his wrist. "Well, we'd better get going."

Rei nodded. "Me, too. Take care."

As she watched them walk away, she was once again grateful for the love her grandparents had always shown her. She opened the door to the restaurant, already planning to order a glass of champagne and the most decadent chocolate dessert Indigo had to offer in lieu of a real lunch.

AFTER WORK, Rei had a dinner meeting with the Bay Area Barristers Alliance. The group of female attorneys had started off as a study group when they'd attended Boalt. It had been good to see her friends tonight, especially after getting an admonishing phone call from Dr. Solís this afternoon.

Rei hadn't needed the reminder that time was limited. What she'd needed was to be around people. She'd needed to talk and laugh and feel connected. Now, as she started the car, drumming her fingers on the steering wheel, she debated where to go next. She was driving toward Miraloma Park, but the quiet solitude of her house didn't appeal right now.

She let her mind drift back to that night. She'd been unable to stop thinking about Chris, about the delicious taste of his kiss, the searing heat of his touch. She shifted subtly in her seat as the mental images caused an all too physical reaction.

Her other reaction was purely emotional and it surprised her. They'd only met four days ago—how could she possibly miss him? And yet there was no denying that she'd woken up this morning cuddling the spare pillow and wishing it were him.

Turning the Lexus into a parking space on Market Street, she pulled her cell phone from her purse. She dialed a number that she hadn't had long enough that she should have memorized it. Chris answered on the second ring.

"Hi. It's Jade."

"I was just thinking about you."

She could hear the smile in his voice and the sound of it uncoiled the tension she hadn't been aware of in her chest. "Oh, really? What were you thinking?"

"Actually, it was more like remembering and wondering. I was remembering the warm scent of flowers on your skin and how hot you felt in my arms. How you tasted when we kissed and how you whimpered when I touched you a certain way, how wet you got."

Rei leaned her head back on the driver's seat and closed her eyes. Her pulse accelerated as his words and images seduced her. This was what she needed, to forget everything except the demands of her body. "And?"

"I'm rock hard right now and remembering how it felt to be buried inside of you, to feel you clench around my cock and call out my name when I made you come. And—"

She gasped softly as desire pooled between her thighs. Oh, yeah. She remembered that, too. Vividly. "And...?"

"And I was wondering when I would see you again. When can I have you again?"

"Is now a good time?"

"Now?" She'd surprised him but he recovered quickly. "Now is the best time."

She smiled at the husky emphasis he put on the word "best." "I'm in the Financial District—where's the best place to meet?"

"Since you're close to the Bay Bridge, why don't you just come to my place in Oakland?"

Rei hesitated. This was supposed to be uncommitted sex with no real life overlap. Meeting at his home was more intimate than a hotel, so much more personal.

His voice was low and seductive in her ear. "You're already in the car, so let's cut down on the wait time. I promise to make it worth the drive when you get here."

"I know you will." She laughed softly even as her body thrummed in anticipation. Scribbling on the notepad she pulled from inside the dashboard, she wrote down the directions he gave. "I'm on my way."

She was about to hang up when he spoke again. "What are you wearing? I want to fantasize about the clothes you'll be stripping off in a few minutes."

Rei looked down at her oxford cloth shirt and light wool trousers. And she didn't even want to think about the plain cotton bra and panties she wore underneath. But there wasn't time to go home to change or to stop and buy something more enticing. So she told the truth and described her attire. "Not exactly sexy, huh?"

"On you, I'll bet it is. Besides, I never told you about my wool fetish."

Rei laughed. "My turn. What are you wearing?"

"I've got on a T-shirt and a pair of jeans. But, by the time you get here, I'll be naked."

LIPSTICK HAD probably been a mistake.

She'd taken the time to paint on a dark peach gloss she'd found in her purse. However, in the next few minutes she'd either chew it off in nervousness or Chris would smear it off when he kissed her. Applying the lip color had been as much a waste of time as securing her hair in a chignon when she was only going to let it down again.

Why the hell was she nervous anyway? She stepped into the elevator and stood near the wall, remembering how she'd made Chris do the same thing at the hotel. It should have calmed her, knowing that he wanted her, knowing that he waited for her. Sex was a sure thing and, based on their last encounter, so was satisfaction. So why did she feel so anxious?

Rei walked up to the address Chris had given her and saw an envelope taped to the door. Her name— or rather Jade's—was printed in a bold, sure hand on the front. Inside was a note that read, 'I'm glad you're here. The door is unlocked. Come on in and be prepared to come a lot.' She smiled at the sexual arrogance but also the warmth that suddenly filled her.

She turned the knob and stepped eagerly into the entryway. Dozens of bright spotlights shone down from tracks on the high ceiling. Soulful jazz music drifted softly from a stereo somewhere, both calming and seducing her. There was another note on the floor with only an arrow pointing deeper into the loft.

Rei walked further inside, her heels clicking on the hardwood, and glanced around curiously. To her right was a rustic-looking Italian kitchen; to the left an ornately dramatic French Provincial dining room. Ahead she could see that the living room was decorated with British Colonial pieces while the office area was strictly modern.

She stopped in her tracks, bemused by the schizophrenic mix of styles. The eclectic décor made her wonder if Chris had serious commitment issues. Shaking her head, Rei looked down to find another paper arrow. This one directed her to the circular staircase near the wall of windows overlooking the city.

She made her way up the steps and finally rounded a half wall that opened onto a deep, carpeted room. Here the only light came from a gas fireplace and the candles illuminating the animal print motif. She stifled a giggle when she saw the zebra striped throw rugs and leopard spot armchair. Good grief, this man had awful taste.

At her feet was a long arrow made of silver foil condom packets. Giggling aloud, she looked over to see that the unusual sign pointed to the king-size bed. Chris was lying on the mattress with a tiger print sheet draped over his lap and a grin on his handsome face.

"Welcome to the jungle."

Rei laughed heartily. "You need to fire your decorator."

He gave a good-natured shrug. "I can't. She's my sister."

"You Tarzan, me unimpressed."

"You're also overdressed. Do something about that, will you?"

She tossed her purse onto the leopard chair and toed off her pumps. Rei unfastened her trousers and slid them down her hips, along with her underwear. Kicking the pants aside, she watched Chris's face, saw the quickening rise and fall of his bare chest. In the firelight, she watched him watching her. She saw the desire in his expression...and in the tented shape of the bed sheet.

Tilting her head, she smiled at him and reached up to pull the clip from her hair, releasing it to flow over her shoulder. Letting the sexy wail of the saxophone on the stereo set the pace, she undid her shirt, one button at a time. With a quick snap of the front hook, she opened her bra and let both articles slide off her shoulders to the floor.

She stood before him, her breathing rapid and her limbs heavy. A quiver of excitement darted through her body, settling between her legs with electric anticipation. You'd think it was their first time together. But having had him before only made her want him more.

"Come over here, lady."

His voice was hoarse with lust. She walked toward him with confident steps, her hips swaying seductively, her attitude a blend of temptation and intention.

His blood sizzled in his veins and his shaft thickened against the sheet. Damn, she was beautiful.

Yet there was something else in her eyes, the barest hint of uncertainty, which made her look soft and fragile. Tonight she looked more like the woman from the dating service than the exotic temptress from the nightclub. His protective instinct surfaced and he wondered who the real Rei Davis was. He wondered if she knew.

She climbed onto the bed and he pulled the sheet away so that he could feel her against him. He rested his weight on his left elbow, opening his other arm to embrace her. Their naked bodies aligned so that her firm breasts pressed against his chest and her thighs touched his belly. She smoothed her left palm over his bare chest, leaving a trail of heat in the wake of her touch.

While she nuzzled her lips against his throat, he took pleasure in running his fingers through her long silky hair. Then he cupped her cheek with his right hand and settled his mouth over hers. The first brush of her lips against his mouth had him wanting to devour her. But he held back until she opened to him with a sigh of abandon.

He welcomed the thrust of her tongue, letting her explore his mouth in lazy circles. Then she deepened the kiss, unleashing a little of the need he felt. He tasted her excitement and responded in kind, turning the kiss urgent and demanding.

With his free hand, he began a slow, seductive exploration, seeking to rediscover her erogenous zones, those secret places like the nape of her neck where she loved to be stroked and caressed. He trailed his fingers lower until he cupped a smooth, firm breast in his palm and felt her shiver in response.

He kneaded his thumb across her nipple while tracing the same pattern on her tongue. Then he broke the kiss to bend his head and take the beaded tip into his mouth. The flick of his tongue on the engorged flesh made her quiver and arch closer as he suckled each breast in turn. The way she was wiggling against him drove him nuts.

Grasping his face, she pulled him up to capture his lips again. He trailed his fingers down her back, along her smooth buttock then around to the juncture of her thighs. She gasped against his mouth as he slipped one, two fingers into her heat. She was so wet, so ready. He felt her body clamp down on his hand while she kissed him like her life depended on it.

She moaned low and deep, and grasping his hair in her fists, she tugged his head down. Knowing exactly what she wanted, he obeyed her silent command and slid toward the end of the bed. He placed hot kisses on her abdomen and belly before kneeling on the floor to trace wet patterns along the inside of her thigh.

When his tongue delved inside her, she half gasped, half groaned at the first touch of his mouth to her damp, swollen flesh. He clasped her knees and pushed her legs further apart. Her fingers dug into the muscles of his shoulders as she arched her hips, silently begging him for more.

He obliged with slow, sensuous laps of his tongue from her silken folds all the way to the burgeoning crest. Now his hands were holding her down as she thrashed on the bed. Suckling gently and listening to her quickly escalating cries, he coaxed her toward a climax against his mouth.

"Ooh wow, Chris. That was—oh wow."

"We're not done. I promised to make it worth the drive, remember. But you only came once."

She stared at his raging erection with a wicked smile. "You'll have to try *harder* next time."

"Honey, I don't think I can get any harder."

She crooked her finger and grinned. "Then come here so I can kiss it all better."

He stood up as she swung her legs to sit on the edge of the bed. Sliding her hands over his butt, she opened her mouth and took him between her soft, moist lips. He had to grit his teeth to keep from shouting out loud as she nibbled and licked him. The sensation of her hot, greedy mouth was beyond incredible and he craved the sweet release that beckoned.

More than that, though, he wanted the sensation of joining. He wanted to be inside her the next time she came. After gently, and regretfully, pulling away, Chris rushed across the bedroom to grab a condom off the carpet. After protecting them, he propelled himself back onto the mattress and positioned himself at her entrance.

He plunged into her. Overwhelmed by the sensation of hot wet heat, he increased the friction. She scored his sweat-slick back with her nails as he rocked them toward release. Slipping his palms beneath her hips, he pulled her closer still and buried himself to the hilt.

Her pelvis swiveled in almost frantic circles as he pleasured her. He'd only begun and already she was coming again. He fought his own desire, wanting to make it good for her, but in the end he lost control. Arching his back, he groaned and quickly exploded inside her.

A few moments later they lay side by side, drowsy and spent. Chris had gutted the candles but left the fireplace going. He watched the glow of the flames dance on Rei's golden skin as he lazily stroked his fingers over damp shoulder.

"Will you stay?"

She was lying on her stomach, her head pillowed on her folded arms, and barely opened her eyes to answer. "I've got to be at work in the morning."

"So do I, but that's why alarm clocks were invented."

She seemed to consider it, though her features were oddly set. "No, I don't think so."

He wasn't surprised by her refusal, but that hadn't stopped him from hoping. He hid his disappointment with effort. "Let me guess. You snore? You talk in your sleep?"

"Yep. I also hog the covers."

He could tell that her humor was strained and decided to let it drop. "Okay, then at least let me offer you a quick shower."

He felt her relax beneath his hand, obviously relieved by the change of subject. She opened her eyes to offer him a genuine smile. "Mmm, hot water, slick soap and a gorgeous guy? That I'll gladly take."

Chris forced himself to smile back, confused by the tightness in his chest. He'd walked into this situation with the knowledge that she didn't want anything serious. Rei wouldn't tolerate anything non sexual from him, but damned if for some reason he didn't want to give it. He believed the compatibility software and he believed his own instincts.

Rei both intrigued and confounded him. She was so sexy and inviting one minute and the next she shut emotional doors in his face. He wasn't even sure why he wanted them opened—those doors would only close behind her when she left. But he wasn't interested in dating any other women. He had his hands full with Rei and "Jade" and wanting them to be one and the same.

8

REI STOOD in the bathroom in her bra and panties, running Chris's comb through her hair to untangle the long strands. Their quick shower had actually turned into a half hour of wonderful wet sex. She was looking forward to her daily yoga routine tomorrow to loosen her sore muscles.

Chris had already dried off and tugged on a pair of briefs. He leaned against the bathroom door, watching her. "So, you won't stay. But will you come back?"

"What do you mean? Tomorrow?" She looked over at him while she worked out a particularly stubborn knot.

"Yes, I want to see you again."

The timbre of his voice alerted her to what he was really asking, but she deliberately misunderstood in hopes of avoiding the issue. "Sure. I'm not going to turn down an offer of incredible sex."

"How about doing something outside of the bedroom?"

Rei wriggled her eyebrows at him. "Ooh, that sounds like fun. Maybe on the dining table or in that rocking chair in the living room?"

He startled, then laughed despite himself. "Well, I was thinking of using the dinner table but I'd plan to cook you a meal."

"Thanks, but no." When he stiffened at her sharp response, she made an effort to soften her tone. "We had a great time. Let's leave it at that, okay?"

Chris stared at her, an odd expression in his eyes, one that she couldn't decipher. But it made her feel guilty and wrong nonetheless. She focused her gaze on the tile floor and began to braid her hair so it wouldn't be a bird's nest in the morning.

"Why do you keep pushing me away?"

His voice sounded tight, as if he were barely holding his temper, causing her to glance over. Now she recognized the look. Like she'd disappointed him... That was it. It was the same kind of look her father had given her. And she resented it as much from Chris as from Gordon.

Deciding to forget about braiding her hair, she pushed past him into the bedroom to get dressed. "I've got to go."

He sighed heavily and turned in the doorway. He crossed his arms over his bare chest, a slight frown tugging at his mouth. "When—?"

"I don't know. I'll call you."

Chris straightened and came toward her as she hastily buttoned her shirt. "This isn't fair, Jade. We agreed to explore our desires and have some fun together, but you're treating me like some hired stud. What, I'm good enough to screw but not good enough to talk to?"

Rei flinched at his coarse accusation. Knowing it was true added to her guilt, but damn it, having to negotiate these sensitive waters was exactly why she wanted to keep it physical.

"You said you weren't looking to get involved or start a relationship. You agreed that this, whatever it is, wouldn't affect our real lives, that there would be no complications."

God, she absolutely did not need any complications, not now when everything was so uncertain.

"I've changed my mind."

His voice was a harsh whisper, hinting at things she didn't want to deal with. Rei shoved her feet into her shoes and reached for her purse. "I'm sorry, Chris. I haven't changed mine. This is not going anywhere except toward a bad ending."

He forcibly pushed away from the wall and came at her. "Of course it's not going anywhere. You've already resolved not to let it." He stopped beside her, close enough for her to smell his freshly showered skin, but didn't touch her. "All I'm asking you for is a real date, not a June wedding. Come on, Jade, take a risk. Meet me for lunch tomorrow."

She looked over at him finally and felt the emotional punch right in her gut. His face, already handsome, was all the more appealing for the stubborn expression of hope. The firelight turned Chris's green eyes to a warm gold, adding shadows and depth to his gaze, promising things she didn't dare accept....

CHECKING IN
I was thinking about you so I thought I'd say hi. Hi.
DCL3

RE: CHECKING IN
Hi. It's after midnight. What are you doing online?
RLD49

RE: UP LATE
Same as you, I guess. Not sleeping.
I had a date tonight, but it didn't go exactly as I'd hoped. This getting-to-know-you stage is hard, isn't it?
DCL3

RE: NOT SLEEPING
Oh, you've gone out with someone already? Me, too, and my night didn't end well either.
Actually, my day didn't start well. It's been one of those emotionally confrontational days that keeps replaying in my mind. With everything else that's going on, this is probably the worst time to get involved in a new relationship.
RLD49

RE: OPEN COMMUNICATION
Want to talk about it?
One thing I've noticed is that with a company like Lunch Meetings, where you log in on a secure server, the Internet provides a unique type of privacy. No one can see you or find out anything about you that you don't tell them. That means you can remain anonymous while being as open and honest as you want.
Sometimes that's the best way to get something off your chest, like striking up a conversation with a stranger on a plane during a long flight.
DCL3

Chris stared at the computer screen, watching for the little envelope icon to appear. But after checking twice, he still had no new messages. Maybe he'd pushed too hard. Just when he figured she wouldn't answer, though, the computer chimed.

RE: STRANGERS ON A PLANE
I only signed up for Lunch Meetings because my best friend talked me into it. There have been too many disappointments in the past, too many times when the man in my life let me down. So now it's hard for me to trust.
I can't believe I'm telling you all this. And now that I've bared my soul, I guess this is the last time I'll hear from you.
RLD49

RE: MEN AREN'T CREATED EQUAL
You're assuming your past experiences are the
norm instead of the exception and painting every
man with the same brush. But the funny thing
about trust is you've got to give it to get it.
The key is to be truthful about who you are and what
you want. Instead of anticipating the worst, why
not take a chance and be open to the possibilities?
DCL3

RE: TAKING CHANCES
Thanks for listening. I'll think about what you've said.
I have a couple of things to do before I go to
sleep, so I'll say good night.
RLD49

RE: LISTENING
That's what air travel friends are for. Talk to you later.
DCL3

Chris leaned back in his desk chair, staring out the
picture window into the night. The cell phone he'd
laid on the desk began to ring. He looked at the clock
on his laptop screen then took a deep breath and
answered the call.

"Hello?"

"It's me."

He silently exhaled, closing his eyes in relief at the
sound of Rei's soft voice.

"Am I disturbing you?"

Chris rubbed his temples. "If by 'disturb' you mean unsettle, fascinate and arouse, then, yes. You disturb the hell out of me."

He could hear her breath against the receiver. Then she suddenly spoke in a rush. "My cell phone number is 555-8921 and my text pager is 555-7949. I'll see you at lunch."

He listened to the dial tone for a second after she'd hung up and then set the phone on its cradle.

It's a date.

Wednesday, April 16th

Accomplishments: Get in touch with old friends; Try some new types of food

REI STARTLED when she felt the vibrations. The humming sensation sent little tingles of pleasure over her skin.

She hoped no one had noticed the quiet electronic buzz under her bench. Reaching beneath her robe, she pulled her pager off its clip. While the petitioner's attorney presented his case, she glanced down at the tiny LCD screen. Chris was text messaging her again.

SO HOT 4 U :-P

Rei hid a smile and touched the button to store the message. The little panting face was definitely mutual, but she couldn't think about that right now. She was adjudicating a case.

Robert Cote settled his features in what he must have assumed was a sympathetic expression. "Your Honor, my client loves her children and wants only the best for them. But she is a hard working woman with numerous responsibilities…"

He rambled on, extolling his client's virtues. When Rei felt another vibration against her thigh. She lifted the pager slightly off her lap to read the message.

WHATCHA WEARING? ;-)

She had to rotate the pager to realize the little face was winking this time. After storing that message as well, she made a mental note to call him during her next break. If she ever got one. Why did people insist on coming to court instead of just talking things out?

"Okay here's the deal. Mrs. O'Neal the second can adjust her work hours so that she can feed Amy and Brian in the morning and see them off to school."

"But—"

Rei kept speaking right over the beginnings of a protest. "Mrs. O'Neal the first can pick the kids up from school, make sure they do their homework and feed them dinner if necessary while they wait for their mother."

"But—"

Rei talked over the second protest. "That's it.

That's my decision." She banged her gavel and nodded to Mary Alice. "I'll be back in five minutes."

She stepped out of the courtroom and into her chambers, flipped open her cell phone and dialed Chris's number. "What's on your mind, as if I have to ask?"

"You. Naked. With me. Also naked. I put the giraffe print sheets on the bed for you."

"Oh, I can just picture them." Rei laughed at the mental image. "I'll bet they're just as awful as the rest of the room."

"I'll ignore that. What else can you picture?"

Responding to the playfulness in his voice, she said, "You. Naked."

"With you?"

She closed her eyes, picturing his big, lean-muscled body lounging on his bed. "No, you're alone."

Chris growled into the phone. "You're mean."

"And you're hard, incredibly hard."

He breathed heavily. "Yeah, I really am. And you're not here."

"Sure, I am." Rei opened her eyes long enough to glance over and make sure her chamber door was shut, then put herself back into the fantasy. "I'm sitting in the leopard chair, watching you."

"Voyeurism? Really? I think I'd be shocked if I wasn't so turned on." There was laughter in his voice but also a hint of fascination.

She was a little shocked herself, but figured she

could blame it on her hormones. "Not half as turned on as I am seeing you touch yourself like that."

"Like what?" Chris's voice deepened and he cleared a rasp from his throat. "Tell me what you want me to do."

In her mind she saw his large hand grasp his shaft, saw the lust in his green eyes and the invitation in his smile. "A light touch to begin with, I think. Long, lazy caresses up and down."

"Uh huh. What are you doing?"

She easily pictured him stroking himself, an incredibly erotic image, so her voice was breathless when she answered. "I can't take my eyes off of you and I'm soo wet."

"Watching you watching me is one of the sexiest things I've ever seen. Are you touching yourself?"

"Um, yes. I've draped my legs over the arms of the chair. My thighs are spread wide and I'm using my fingers. If possible, you get even harder so a firmer grip is necessary, faster with more friction."

She heard him groan softly into the phone, his breathing rapid. "Good thing my office door is closed," Chris murmured.

Rei's eyes widened. She had initiated this little game of phone sex, but she never thought he'd actually follow her instructions. "Are you really—?"

Chris sighed, sounding frustrated in the best way. "I'm fully dressed, if that's what you mean. But I'd be lying if I said I didn't wish my hand was yours."

"Mmm, I wish it was, too." She looked up at a

knock on her door. Mary Alice poked her head in and made a "two minutes" signal. "But I have to go back to work now."

"I can't. Not yet anyway."

She gave a completely smug and unsympathetic laugh. "Well, at least I know you'll be thinking about me for a while."

"What makes you think I ever stop?" His voice was rich with desire and humor. "I'll meet you at Zuni Café at noon. I'll be the guy with the big smile on his face."

AT ELEVEN FORTY-FIVE, Chris stood in the triangular two-story entryway admiring the richly colored Indian blankets hanging along the white adobe walls. Zuni Café, with its Southwestern ambiance and French-Italian cuisine, was one of his favorite restaurants in San Francisco. Hearing his name, he turned to see Rei walk through the front door.

He smiled at the sight of her long hair flowing down the back of her bright blue overcoat. When she reached his side, Chris leaned down and kissed her wind-chilled cheek.

"You're early, too, I see."

"I'm right on time, actually. Like a wizard, I arrive exactly when I mean to." Her gaze was as warm as the welcoming smile she sent over her shoulder as she hung up her coat on the rack.

He recognized the reference to the classic J.R.R. Tolkien story instantly and grinned. "You're a *Lord of the Rings* fan. I knew there was a reason I liked you."

"Only one?"

As she turned, he finally noticed her outfit. The colors were conservative, the patterns plain, but something about the way she wore them seemed frankly sensual. The white blouse was draped low enough for him to detect a hint of camisole lace. The hem of her caramel brown skirt ended well above her knees, showing off shapely legs down to her dark chocolate high heels.

"Well, maybe more than one."

A hostess led them past the copper-topped bar and semi-open kitchen with its roaring brick ovens to a table near the floor-to-ceiling windows. They debated the merits of the Jackson *Lord of the Rings* films in comparison with the original Tolkien books while perusing the menu and waiting for their drinks.

When their waitress appeared with tall glasses of iced tea, Chris ordered his usual. "I'll have the hamburger on toasted focaccia bread, medium-rare."

"I'd like to try the deep-fried mixed fruit, the house-cured anchovies with Parmesan, the foie gras and the yaquina oysters on the half shell, please." Rei lowered the menu to find both Chris and the waitress staring at her. But she just smiled brightly and shrugged. "I'm trying new things this week."

He laughed as the waitress left to fill their orders. "I hope you like those appetizers more than you did the tequila."

As they waited for their lunch, Chris engaged her in a conversation about their favorite books and movies, keeping everything light and impersonal while he prepared himself. Finally he inhaled deeply, having realized he'd been anxiously holding his breath.

"There's something I need to tell you." Reaching for Rei's hand, he rubbed his thumb over the back of it. "The sex has been incredible, you know. It's never been as good with anyone else as it is with you." He paused, holding her gaze as firmly as her fingers. "But I want more."

"You want more sex?"

She laughed but he felt her hand tense beneath his.

"Chris, I don't think that will be a problem. I've made no secret about how much you turn me on."

"You have other secrets, though. We both do."

She looked away, taking a long sip of her iced tea. "It's more interesting that way, don't you think?"

"It's easier to control, you mean. I know you didn't want any complications, but I think the rules need to change."

Chris paused while the waitress placed the foie gras and anchovies in front of Rei. As he watched, her expression became anxious. She lifted one of the thin fish, sniffed it then took a small bite. After a wince and a long sip of tea, she scooped up a forkful of the pâté.

"You're trying new things, right? Are you willing to be something more than lovers and strangers?"

"We're not exactly strangers." Rei stalled for time by shoving the foie gras into her mouth. He wasn't sure if the face she made was in response to the topic or the food.

"No, we aren't." He drew another deep breath and braced himself for her reaction. "You wouldn't know this, but I'm named after my father and grandfather. David Christopher London III."

She stared at him, a frozen expression on her face. Her eyes were turbulent, though, when she jerked her hand away. He could see the wheels turning, saw her making the connections, and suddenly he wondered if he'd just made a huge mistake. But, no, he didn't stand a chance in hell if he didn't come clean with her about who he was and what he wanted.

"You're DCL3. You son of a bitch."

"I'm sorry. But I had to tell you before we go any further. I had to be honest—"

"Honest?" She glanced around the restaurant then lowered her voice. "You've been playing me from the very start. All that nonsense about remaining anonymous while being open and honest. When I think about the things I e-mailed you…"

"Things you wouldn't have told me in person, things you didn't trust me enough to share."

Rei scowled at him. "Well, obviously I was right not to trust you."

The waitress chose that moment to deliver the rest of their food. The burger smelled delicious but Chris's stomach was too twisted in knots to even think about eating it. He was a risk taker in sports and in business but not in his personal life. He'd never met a woman he considered worth it before.

Rei waited until they were alone again before she

leaned forward, pointing her index finger at him. "You agreed to the terms that first night at the hotel and then went and violated my privacy."

He stepped around that landmine and chose to address what he thought was the more important issue. "Yeah, I agreed at first, but I also told you last night I'd changed my mind. When you gave me your number, I figured you had, too."

This time she was the one avoiding a trap. "How did you even get my Lunch Meetings e-mail?"

He forced himself to meet her gaze. "I own the service."

She fell back against her seat. "Damn it, I don't believe you. Is this how you operate? You steal information and manipulate the results?"

"Hey, I know you're angry but believe one thing. I've never done this before. I wouldn't jeopardize the reputation of my company or expose my clients. But you—I don't know—you blew me away." Chris leaned forward, willing her to see his sincerity. "I wasn't looking to meet anybody and there you were. Then you were gone. When fate brought you into Lunch Meetings, I saw an opportunity and I took it."

"Why should I believe anything you say? Don't you see how you've betrayed my trust? I thought I was talking to a friend."

"I'll apologize again, because I know I misled you, but I didn't feel like I had a choice, Rei. You wouldn't let me in any other way. Every time we've been together, you've shut me out. This still doesn't have to be complicated, Rei. We'll see each other in and out of bed, and you'll have to learn to say the things you told me online in person. The relationship doesn't have to end, it just changes."

She slumped in her chair and wouldn't look at him. "You lied to me."

Her voice sounded more petulant than irate and he didn't want to fight with her, but Chris felt his own anger was also justified. "When did you plan to tell me your real name, 'Jade'? How long were you going to keep lying to me?"

She blinked several times but didn't answer. Knowing his point was made and not wanting to push her any harder, Chris backed off and concentrated on his own lunch. Rei would definitely walk away now and he had no intention of begging her to see him again. If it was over, let it be a clean break with some of his self-respect intact.

Rei picked up her fork and toyed with hot Concord grapes and peach slices as the last of her anger evaporated into embarrassment. She was so pissed off with Chris.... However she couldn't avoid the truth. She was just as guilty as he and, thinking back to their e-mails, he'd offered her several chances to reveal herself.

Rei tipped the oyster and brine into her mouth, then tossed the empty shell back onto the plate and reached for one of the rolls in the breadbasket to cleanse her palate. The slimy feel of the oyster sliding down her throat was not an experience she cared to repeat, despite the supposed aphrodisiac effects.

That was another truth she had to face. What kind of person was she really, to use him just for sex, never wanting to know more about him, treating him like he was nothing more than a sex toy? She'd wanted to get swept up into a passionate affair, but while sex without any personal connection might be passionate, it wasn't satisfying and it wasn't right.

Her plan had been to break it off as soon as they went too far and Chris had gone as far as he could to make something more of their liaison. But a personal connection was exactly what she wanted to avoid. Despite what Chris had said about being receptive and taking chances, there were too many negative possibilities once she rescheduled the tests for Dr. Solís.

In the meantime though, he hadn't asked for a lifetime or any other type of commitment. There was no reason they couldn't be friends...with benefits. They could continue to be lovers while getting to know each other better. Rei drew a deep breath and apologized.

"I don't know when I would have confessed who I really am. 'Jade' made for such a great shield, you see. With an alter ego I was free to be anybody I wanted, except myself."

Chris wiped a smear of ketchup from the corner of his mouth. "You're an attractive and intriguing woman, Rei. Why would you want to be anyone else?"

She heard the interest and concern in his voice and a part of her wanted to respond. However, she still chose to keep some secrets to herself and so told him only part of the truth.

"I wanted to let my hair down, get a little wild and crazy. It's easier to do that when you're hiding behind a different persona. I didn't need or want to know anything about you, except in bed, because that's the only place Jade existed. That was unfair to you and I'm sorry."

"I accept your apology, Rei, if you'll accept mine."

She looked up to see hope and understanding in his light green eyes. Smiling, she held out her hand. "Hi, I'm Rei Davis. I'm a commissioner in the Unified Family Court. My interests include travel, romance novels and NFL football."

He gently gripped her fingers. "Hi, Rei. My name is Chris London. I own a dating service, I like to swim and play golf and go to jazz concerts."

"This is weird, isn't it? On the one hand, I shouldn't trust you because you deceived me. But if you hadn't, I never would have made a new friend."

"Now that we've been introduced, where do we go from here?" Chris must have seen her hesitation because he reached for her hand this time.

"I'll have to think about—"

"Yeah, yeah, you'll call me." He dropped her hand in frustration, crossing his arms over his chest. "I've heard it before—*every* other time you've backed away."

"That's not—"

"Maybe if you'd stop running long enough, you'd see—"

"Hey!" Rei smacked her fingers on the tabletop.

"If you'd stop interrupting me, I could finish what I was going to say."

He kept his arms folded and still wore a disgruntled expression, but he was listening.

"I'll have to think about whether I want to go out with my lover or have sex with my friend. But either way, I'm not only willing but looking forward to spending more time with you."

His frown lifted to a smirk and the smirk quickly turned into the charmingly boyish smile she adored. Chris uncrossed his arms and pulled her toward him for a quick kiss. His appetite apparently restored, he dug into his hamburger with gusto.

Rei wished she were half as enthusiastic about her lunch. Pushing the salted fish, duck liver, fried fruit and bivalves aside, she caught the attention of their server. "Could you please take this away and bring me a garden salad with vinaigrette dressing? Thanks."

PajamaPartyGirl is now online
PajamaPartyGirl is instant messaging you

PajamaPartyGirl: How's it going with the Lunch guy?

JadeBlossom: Good. I mean, we've struck up this weird kind of friendship.

PajamaPartyGirl: I can't invest in the company based on weird friendships. How about the other guys who e-mailed you?

JadeBlossom: Several of them seemed really nice, but I didn't want to lead them on. I think I've found a match and you'll never guess who it is.

PajamaPartyGirl: The guy who kept asking about your shoes. He sounded hot.

JadeBlossom: Ew. Not him. It's the guy I've been seeing.

PajamaPartyGirl: You mean the boy toy is the one you've been e-mailing? How the hell did that happen? I'm confused.

JadeBlossom: So was I. Do you believe in fate?

PajamaPartyGirl: No, and I'm not big on coincidence either. Who is this guy?

JadeBlossom: Chris London. It turns out he owns Lunch Meetings.

PajamaPartyGirl: Oh really. And this doesn't set off any alarms for you?!? By any chance was he there the day we signed up?

JadeBlossom: Yeah, he recognized me, but he was with a client and couldn't break away.

PajamaPartyGirl: I'll bet you're not the only one he recognized. Think about it, Rei. He's trying to get money to expand and you walk in with the heir to Hollinger/Hansen, the folks he's been pitching for funds. I'll admit it could have been a fluke that you met him at Divas, but how do you know the rest of this wasn't a setup from the very beginning?

JadeBlossom: I don't think so, Peej. I'm a good judge of character.

9

MARVIN CARRINGTON LOOKED like a new man. Sort of.

He'd had his hair cut and styled. He wore new glasses and he looked good in a pale blue monochromatic shirt and tie. But the look in his puppy-brown eyes and his body language were the same. He still came across as insecure and slightly desperate.

"I don't know what went wrong, Chris."

"Well, tell me how your date started and we'll figure it out from there."

Marvin shrugged. "Tina asked when I wanted to meet. I said whenever it fit into her schedule. She asked where did I want to go? I told her anyplace she liked. When we got to the coffee shop, I ordered the same thing she did."

Chris kept himself from wincing and instead nodded for Marvin to continue. "How did the conversation go?"

Marvin shrugged again. "I thought I was using open communication. I told her how long it had been since my last date and what went wrong in that relationship. I touched her a lot so she'd know I was sensitive and just tried to show her the real me. She didn't talk much about herself and when I asked if anything was wrong she said nothing, but she kept sighing."

"Okay, Marvin. I think I've heard enough. When a woman says "nothing," it always means "something." That's great that you let her see the real you, but you might have shown her too much you all at once. There are twelve steps to intimacy and you jumped right to step four or five."

He spent the next twenty minutes coaching Marvin and building his self-esteem and then practically held his hand while he called Tina to ask her for another date. When he left Chris's office and headed for the front door, he was walking with a more confident stride and a spring in his step.

"You're in a great mood today, considering all the activity around here today." Lara paused by the bar on her way past.

Chris looked up from getting a can of his favorite energy drink and shrugged. A team of Hollinger/Hansen auditors and risk assessment specialists had been combing through his files all morning, checking the account books and reading client contracts. "Hey, if this is what it takes, let them look to their hearts content."

"I thought all they needed were copies of the company's financial statements and business plan? I don't think all of this probing is typical, Chris."

Given Rei's connection to P.J. Hollinger, he didn't think so, either. But he wasn't going to sweat it. "I heard from Andrew Johnston that the expansion strategy presentation went well. He seemed confident the funding would be approved."

"Let's hope so. My husband wasn't pleased about that private investigator questioning my neighbors," Lara conceded.

Chris was just turning back to his office when he spotted Grant Bronson. His eyes narrowed when he realized Grant was talking to Marvin. Chris walked up to them just in time to hear they'd be at the weekly mixer Friday night.

"See you around, Grant. See you later, Chris, and thanks again."

Grant cocked his head toward Marvin's retreating back. "Is he another one of your personal projects?"

"I told you before, I can't—"

"Talk about your other clients." Grant offered a self-depreciating grin. "Sorry, man. I was just curious."

Chris didn't like the man's curiosity and so kept his tone cool. "What are you doing here? We didn't have an appointment."

"I just stopped by to check my e-mail. I'll see you at the mixer, right?"

He held Grant's too-innocent stare for a second then finally nodded. "Yeah. I'm the host."

"Cool. Catch you later." Grant stuffed his hands into his front pockets and ambled into the computer café.

Chris watched him go, uneasiness settling into his gut. What the hell was that about?

Thursday, April 17th

Accomplishments: Buy flowers for no reason;
Face backwards on an elevator

"CHICKEN SALAD, huh? That's not exactly daring."
Chris ran his finger down the menu. The ever-popular Hayes Street Grill was the setting for their date today. "How about the quail salad with grilled figs?"

Rei rolled her eyes at his teasing. "I don't think so. After yesterday's lunch, I'm taking a day off from my quest for new adventures. What are you going to have?"

"A cheeseburger. You can never go wrong with a burger."

"So, before the waiter came over, you were saying something about your plans for tonight?" Elbows on the table, she rested her chin on her hands.

Chris draped his arm over the back of his chair. "Yeah, I'm having drinks with my dad at this sports bar we like."

"You and your father are close?"

"Dad and I are…friendly. He and my mom split when I was a kid, and I'm a lot closer to her. Until recently, at least. She's started dating somebody but won't tell me anything about him. Nothing." His lips thinned with displeasure, turning down at one corner. "What?"

"Nothing." Rei suppressed her smile at the look on his face, part concerned man, part disgruntled little boy. "There are a lot of reasons your mom may want to keep this man to herself for a while." She shrugged. "She might not think you'll approve or she might be afraid you won't get along."

"She'll never know until she lets me meet him, will she?" Their food arrived and Chris took a vicious bite out of his cheeseburger.

"Well, maybe things are going well, and she just wants to enjoy his company before deciding where the relationship is heading."

He cocked his head and arched a brow. "Is that what you're doing?"

"Yes, but we're talking about your parents, not us." She took a sip of her mineral water. "Does your dad know she's seeing somebody?"

"Yeah, I told him. It was odd how he reacted though." His brows furrowed. "Dad got kind of tense and flustered and then said he hoped things worked out better for her this time."

"That was nice of him. I take it they parted amicably?" She chose a nice sized piece of smoked chicken breast from her salad plate.

"Not really. That's why I was surprised he seemed to care, considering he's the one who walked out."

Jennifer had married Rei's father over twenty years ago, but Rei still remembered with crystal clarity the day she'd become Gordon's wife. "I acted like I didn't give a damn when my father started seeing someone, but inside I was horrified at the idea of my mother being replaced."

Chris eyed her curiously. "Are you sure you

weren't upset over the idea of *you* being displaced? I've been the most important man in my mom's life for a long time, and it feels strange to know there's somebody else in the picture now."

"You're assuming I had a place in my father's heart to begin with." Rei set down her fork on the plate with an audible click.

"I'm sorry." Chris reached over to touch her hand. "I've tried to maintain some kind of relationship with my dad over the years, but he hasn't exactly been a model parent either. I guess that's why I'm cautious about the sudden interest."

"You have your mom though and I had my *sofubo,* my grandparents." Rei smiled even as her heart squeezed in her chest from missing them so much. "My favorite, most precious childhood memories are of their cottage in Japantown."

"Yeah? Tell me about them."

"My mother would take me to have green tea and my grandmother's tempura and rice balls. I spent hours running curious fingers over her silk screens and porcelain dolls. After lunch, my grandfather would help me to make origami cranes or take me to Lafayette Park to fly *ezodaka* paper kites."

"It sounds like you had a great time with them, Rei."

Her *sofubo* and the special times they'd shared, memories colored with tight hugs and plum candies and love, reminded her of what was happening this weekend. "Hey, Chris. Are you doing anything on Saturday?"

Friday, April 18th

Accomplishments: Get a makeover; Sing in public

SHE FELT like a fraud. Everyone else here tonight was genuinely looking to meet new people and hopefully discover that elusive chemistry, which might become a relationship. Since she was already involved with Chris, Rei hadn't wanted to come to the Lunch Meetings mixer but she'd promised P.J. she would check out the event.

She hadn't told Chris she was coming, hoping to surprise him. As she walked out of the cloakroom, Lara Voigt suddenly appeared at her shoulder. "Hi, welcome. This is your first mixer, right? Come on, I'll introduce you to some people."

"Oh, um, you don't have to—"

"Don't be shy. There are a lot of eligible bachelors at the party tonight, and everyone is just as nervous as you."

In the main dining room, the usual tables and chairs had been replaced with food-laden buffets against the wall. Lara briefly explained how speed dating worked, then left Rei to her own devices. She joined the other people wandering from group to group, sharing rapid introductions and concise information about themselves, before moving on. By the sixth or seventh time she'd said, "Hi, Rei Davis. I'm a San Francisco native and I work for the court system," her cheeks were sore from smiling politely.

Her next partner seemed more interested in a hook-up than a date. The good-looking, dark-haired man used his superior height to try and peer down her cleavage, then flashed her a pearly smile. "Hey, beautiful. Grant Bronson. I think you're exactly who I've been looking for."

Before she could retort, Rei suddenly felt Chris's familiar and very welcome presence by her side.

"That's too bad, because she's been looking for me." He slipped a proprietary arm around her waist and smiled down at her. "Hey, beautiful. You look incredible."

Grant took a step back and raised his palms. "Sorry, man. I didn't realize she was the one."

"It's cool. If you'll excuse us?"

Chris's voice was friendly enough, but Rei saw the cold look in his eyes and she was certain Grant had also. "Why don't you just club me over the head and drag me into the nearest cave?"

"In that dress? Don't tempt me."

He led her around to the bar, where a number of people were chatting in groups or dancing to the club music the dj was spinning. Chris caught the bartender's attention. "John, this is Rei. Whatever the lady wants is on the house, okay?"

"Sure thing, boss. What will you have, ma'am?"

Chris grinned at her. "Anything but tequila, right?"

She took a minute to scan her eyes over the vast

display of bottles on the glass shelves behind the bar. "I think I'll try a Skyy Blue martini, please."

While John made her drink, Chris leaned against the gleaming brass rail and gave her a slow once-over. "Have I told you, you look absolutely amazing tonight?"

Rei pretended to pout at the compliment. "Only once."

"Well, it bears repeating. I love what you did to your hair and I really love that dress."

After work she'd gone to the Crocker Galleria near Union Square. At the pricey salon P.J. had recommended, after a lot of deep breaths and assurances from the stylist, she'd had six inches cut off her hair. It now had lots of layers and fell just to shoulder length. Her head felt lighter and she loved the way her hair swung when she moved, but it was strange not to feel her hair against her back.

While she was at the shopping mall, she'd gone into one of the exclusive apparel stores and splurged on the lavender silk cocktail dress. Triple spaghetti straps crossed one shoulder, leaving the other bare, while the fluted hem brushed the middle of her thighs. Rei slid onto an empty bar stool, careful to keep her knees together.

She took a sip of her cocktail. The heated kick of the ice-cold vodka, combined with her new haircut and first bikini wax, made her feel edgy and warm and daring. "I'll tell you a little something about this dress."

"What's that?"

She leaned close, brushing her lips against his cheek as she whispered her naughty secret. "There's nothing underneath it except an itty bitty pair of thong panties."

His light-green eyes darkened with desire and he groaned softly. "Don't tell me that now. I have to work the crowd and keep them encouraged and entertained."

Rei slid her calf along his pants leg. "Sorry, honey. I didn't mean to distract you from your work. You run along and I'll just sit here and wait for you."

He glanced around then stroked his fingers along the underside of her thigh. "I'll be back. Soon. Very soon."

She twisted sideways on the bar stool and scanned the crowd. The overly enthusiastic dj was cajoling people to get up and sing, but no one exactly leapt at the chance. "Come on, guys, I know some of you dreamed of singing lead for a 1980s hair band. No? Ladies? Are there any divas in the house tonight? Come on, I find that hard to believe."

Maybe it was the word divas, reminding her of the night she met Chris, or maybe it was the alcohol. Maybe it was just her inner bad girl spurring her to risk embarrassment and stage fright while crossing another item off her Life List. But Rei found herself raising her arm.

"I'll try it."

After quickly thumbing through the list of karaoke tunes, she chose "The Greatest," one of her all-time favorite songs. Then it was time to take the stage and

Rei suddenly regretted that martini. She stood nervously in front of the microphone while all eyes in the room seemed to be watching her. As her stomach did an anxious somersault, she closed her eyes.

Pretending she was a girl again, standing in PJ's pink bedroom crooning into a hairbrush, Rei listened for her cue. She was no Whitney Houston, that was for sure. But as the music started, she gave it all she had, from the first line about believing children are our future to the last long-held note about finding strength in love. Grinning widely, she opened her eyes as the crowd cheered and took a dramatic bow.

"That was great!" Chris was clapping loudest of all. He handed her down the steps then gave her a hug. He drew her away from the stage and leaned close to murmur in her ear. "You've never looked more vibrant, and I've never wanted you more."

The proof of his admiration was nudging her leg, but she shook her head. "It's your party, we can't leave."

"No, but we can sneak away. Wait one minute then follow me to the back of the building."

Rei watched the next brave soul get up on stage and try to belt out "Old Time Rock and Roll" while easing her way back through the crowd. Walking out of the bar area, she saw Chris waiting by the offices. But instead of ushering her inside, he guided her further along the hallway and into the storage room.

"The first place anyone might look for me is my office." He closed the door behind them before flipping the light switch.

"And this is so much more romantic, making out next to the work table covered in copy paper and advertising brochures."

"Romance is wherever you make it." He pulled her into his arms and lifted her to the table's edge.

"I thought—" She gasped as he leaned over to nuzzle the side of her neck. Damp heat pooled between her thighs and both nipples beaded in response to his touch. "I thought you had to keep your clients entertained."

"I've found a better way to be entertained."

He reached behind her to unzip her dress. Sliding it from her shoulders and down to her waist, his right hand cupped her left breast and began drawing an intriguing pattern around her nipple. Then he bent down to lick her sensitive flesh, gently nipping the engorged bud with the edge of his teeth.

She groaned and threaded her fingers through his hair, holding him against her. Chris's mouth moved along the erogenous zones on her upper body back to her lips and she met his kiss with equal passion. She teased him, darting her tongue in and out of his mouth in imitation of the way she wanted him to make love to her.

Without breaking contact, he lifted her up just enough to tug her panties down her legs until they hung precariously from one ankle. His questing fingers slid along her skin until he reached the apex of her thighs and his hand stilled.

Rei grinned. "Surprise."

"I love surprises." Chris captured her mouth again in an ardent kiss as his fingers explored every centimeter of her now smooth, hairless labia.

After undoing his belt and pulling down his zipper, she reached inside his pants. Wrapping her hand around his long, hard shaft, she began stroking him at the same pace his fingers were pleasuring her. Her body wept with need as his fingers delved deeper into her sodden heat.

"I want you, Chris. Now, please, right now."

"Anything, everything, the lady wants."

He shoved his pants and briefs down and reached for her. Bracing her hands behind her on the table, she crossed her ankles behind his back while he gripped her hips and drove himself into her. At first he set a slow, deliberate pace and she reveled in the exquisite pleasure of having him inside of her.

When she moaned against his lips at the feel of him sliding in and out, he drew her knees up and began to rock faster, harder and deeper. She felt the gathering tension in her womb and heard his rapidly louder groans. The rolling contractions of her orgasm had her crying out his name and a moment later, he came as well.

Chris held her against his shoulder while they both caught their breath. A few moments later, he kissed her gently and moved aside to let her get down from the table and fix her clothes while he pulled up his pants. After zipping her dress, he wrapped his arm around her waist and pulled her to him.

"It was nice mixing and mingling with you."

"Yeah, I'm really glad I came tonight." Rei laughed and kissed him deeply.

When they broke apart several breathless minutes later, Chris returned to the party while Rei took a compact from her purse and attempted to fix her makeup. She smiled to herself as she reapplied her lipstick. Making love in the middle of a party hadn't even been on her List.

Neither had been falling in love.

Chris was so much more than a great lover. He was charming and sweet and patient, more patient than she deserved maybe. Despite the short time she'd known him, she cherished his insight and laughter and tenderness, his charm and friendship and spontaneity.

A little place in her heart expanded with a feeling she shouldn't allow. Chris had unlocked the door. Now she had to choose whether or not to walk through it. The other side was fraught with uncertainty and the chance of being badly hurt. But she finally had to admit that it might just be worth the risk.

SATURDAY WAS a beautiful warm day but—typically for San Francisco—kind of windy, especially standing on Webster Bridge, the pedestrian walkway over Geary Street. Chris smiled down at Rei, noticing how the sun lit her dark hair and cast a golden glow over her skin. She looked happy and he hoped that being with him was part of the reason.

"Considering how strictly you've been adhering to the ground rules, I was surprised that you asked me out on a non-sex, non-lunch date."

She glanced at him and then away, bright color suddenly warming her cheeks. "I haven't come to this festival in years and I just thought you'd like to see it."

Chris merely smiled, but inside he was pleased that she hadn't denied their change of status. He didn't know when it had happened and often, like when she fell into a melancholy silence and held him at a distance, he didn't know why, but he had fallen for this complex and fascinating woman.

Her sensuality heated his dreams while her compassion toward the kids she worked with touched his heart. He hated the way she still kept a part of herself hidden, admired her willingness to try new things and loved her ability to surprise him. Basically, he was crazy about her.

But he didn't know if Rei returned his feelings and he wasn't going to ask. The least invested person in any relationship had control of the relationship. If he tried too hard to hold her, he'd lose her for sure. It might be better to let her go now, before he got in any deeper. Before she walked out and took his heart with her.

They stood side by side, waiting for the parade to begin. Hundreds of people lined Post Street, the older sitting on folding chairs, the younger standing on the curb, and the youngest bouncing around complaining, 'When is it going to start? Has it started yet? Well, when?'

"So tell me what's going on? Even though I moved here as a kid, I've never been to the Cherry Blossom Festival before."

She raised her voice to be heard over a man on a PA system saying something in Japanese. "The *sakura matsuri* is a celebration of seasonal rebirth. The delicate pink and white flowers only last for a week or two before they fall from the trees. They symbolize the brevity of human life and therefore remind us to rejoice and reflect."

An elderly but spry-looking Japanese man sitting in front of them turned his head to speak to Rei. When she leaned down to reply, he said something else and she laughed. The man patted her arm and winked at Chris before shifting his attention to the first parade vehicles and marching bands coming around the corner.

Chris leaned close to murmur in her ear, "What was so funny?"

"This gentleman overheard what I told you. He said the secret to appreciating life is to stay young. When I asked how to do that, he said you must walk every day, laugh every day and make love every day."

Chris drew his fingers over a sensitive spot on the side of her neck and smiled down at her in a way that made her blush. "I could live by that advice."

"Yes, I somehow guessed that about you."

She wrapped her arms around his waist, stroking his back beneath his lightweight jacket. Rising up on her toes, she pursed her lips for a kiss. Happy to oblige, he leaned down to meet her and covered her mouth with his own. It was a different kind of kiss, more warm than hot and more statement than question. He liked it.

He turned her around, holding her sexy little body against his larger one to block the wind. The street was jam-packed with people, mostly families and friends by the look of them, cheering at dancers in traditional kimono and brightly colored floats as they passed by.

"I used to come every year, especially after my mom died. My *obasaan,* my grandmother, would make shrimp-flavored rice cakes for us to eat while we waited for the parade to start. Afterwards, *Ojiisan,* my grandfather, used to buy me a bonsai tree to remember the day."

Chris wrapped his arms a little tighter around her shoulders in a hug and kissed the top of her hair.

The air filled with the sound of cheering and the deep thundering boom of *taiko* drummers as the Cherry Blossom Queen and her court waved from atop their flower-draped float. As they passed, Rei pointed out the *mikoshi,* or portable shrines, and the *buyo* classical and *minyo* folk dancers.

The parade finally ended with the Taru Mikoshi, a huge barrel-shaped shrine carried by almost a hundred people. Chris followed Rei as she wove through the crowd and walked over to the Japan Center, a five-acre complex at Post and Fillmore streets.

In the Peace Plaza, located between two halves of the Japan Center, Rei pointed out a three-story white pagoda; a wooden drum tower that spanned the entrance to the mall and the copper-roofed Peace Walkway between the Tasamak and Kintetsu buildings.

The sound of drumming and Asian music echoed off the buildings. Lining the large slate tiles were outdoor stages showcasing martial arts demonstrations and traditional dancing and awning-covered kiosks offering Japanese foods and crafts. The scent of stir-fried vegetables in soy sauce and grilled fish filled the cool air.

"Are you hungry, Chris?"

"Starving, actually." He pulled her to his side and leaned in for a quick kiss. "I always seem to be hungry around you."

"Mmm, that can be dessert. For now I'll take you to one of my favorite restaurants. It's on the second floor of Kintetsu Mall."

Miyaki looked like the kind of Japanese house he'd seen in the movies. The tiny restaurant's décor consisted of mat-covered floors, low tables and rice-paper screen walls. However it wasn't as crowded as he'd expected. Most people were probably still out in the Plaza, so they were quickly shown to their seats.

Chris had just adjusted his seat cushion, folding his long legs more comfortably under the short tabletop when his cell phone rang. "Excuse me a second, Rei. It's my sister. Hello?"

"I need you. Can you come over?" Diana's voice sounded thick, like she'd been crying.

He glanced at Rei. "Um, now? Because I'm with—"

"Yes, now, Chris. Mom, Drea and Dad are all on their way." Her voice broke on a fresh sob. "Gabriel is in trouble. Michael and I don't know what to do. Please. You're the only one he ever listens to."

"I'll be there as soon as I can, Di." He hung up and looked at Rei's curious expression. "I'm really sorry about this, but I've got to go."

TO: RLD49
FROM: C_London@email.com (via text pager)
RE: QUICK EXIT
I'm sorry I had to leave so abruptly this afternoon. It looks like my sister and her husband may be headed for a nasty divorce and my nephew is caught in the middle.
He's been getting into trouble at school and Diana caught him smoking. My nephew got suspended from school and refuses to talk to his parents about what happened. I'll be here at my sister's pretty much the rest of the evening.
Otherwise I would have taken you up on that bubble bath. I'd have offered to scrub your back. And your front. Top to bottom. I really like your bottom.
Chris

RAINCHECK
Sometimes, especially in a divorce situation, kids need to have an adult they can trust. I'm sure he'll tell you what's going on and you can help his parents figure out what to do.

I'm home if you want to talk later. Or come share some bubbles.
Rei

Monday, April 21st

Accomplishments: None

REI PARKED her car in the garage, gathered her brief-case of files and walked toward the courthouse lobby. She made a mental note to try to reach Chris this morning. He'd called last night to let her know that his nephew was sleeping over at his place, but then she hadn't heard anything more.

As she approached the door, her court services clerk rushed forward with a look of relief and grabbed her by the elbow.

"Mary Alice? What—?"

"You don't want to go in there, Commissioner." Mary Alice was twice her age and half her weight, but still managed to strong-arm Rei away from the entrance and toward the opposite side of the garage. "There are reporters crawling through all of the corridors, and Judge Orr wants to see you right away."

"Why? What's happened? Thank you." One of the maintenance staff held the service elevator door until they got in, then pushed the button for their floor. Rei turned to Mary Alice. "What in the world is going on?"

Her clerk patted her arm, but her expression was

inscrutable. "The Youth Guidance Center is on level three lockdown. There was a riot among the general population, apparently gang related. Bruce Grayson was involved."

She felt her heartrate increase, certain she didn't want to hear any more. "How?"

"Apparently, he instigated a fight, provoking rivals of his brother's gang. It got…out of hand."

Rei took a deep breath then slowly exhaled. "Tell me."

"Fourteen boys in the medical facility. One guard was taken to the hospital in critical condition after Bruce Grayson stabbed him. They don't think the guard is going to make it."

10

DESPITE THE ATTEMPT at deception, Rei still had to run the media gauntlet. Television and newspaper reporters crowded the hallway, and it didn't take them long to spot her coming down the service corridor. She longed to jump back into the elevator and make her escape, but she had to face them in order to get to the supervising judge's chambers.

"Commissioner Davis, over here!"

"Do you regret your decision?"

"Care to make a statement, Commissioner Davis?"

"Commissioner, do you feel responsible?"

Rei lifted a hand in front of her face to keep the camera lights from blinding her. Mary Alice and Bill Travis, one of the security guards, were doing their best to shield her, but she felt every shouted question like a physical blow. By the time she'd pushed her way through the mob to the presiding judge's office, she felt battered as well as heart sore.

This was her fault. Fifteen people had been adversely affected by her decision; fifteen people had been hurt by her choice. Maybe sixteen. Because, while she took responsibility for her actions, she also felt like a victim. Had Bruce Grayson completely suckered her?

Bill and Mary Alice waited outside, leaving Rei to enter Judge Orr's chambers alone. He sat at his desk, scratching notes on a legal pad, but looked up as she came in. His craggy face appeared more stern than usual and Rei took it as a bad sign when she wasn't invited to sit.

"I assume you know about the situation at the YGC." It was a statement, rather than a question. "Your decision in the case will be reviewed, of course."

Rei's stomach clenched. In the wake of another judge's personal misconduct, she had no doubts as to the scrutiny she was about to come under. It was bad enough she was questioning herself. Now each and every decision would be open to criticism.

"As for your other cases, I'd suggest a zero-tolerance policy—hold firm and if need be fix it later. For now, I think it would be better to err on the cautious side. All right, Commissioner Davis, that's all. Except to remind you that your only comment to the press should be 'no comment.'"

Rei nodded stiffly. "Yes, sir."

She turned and walked out, keeping her head down and her mouth shut as she fought her way to her own chambers. She thanked Bill, who promised to get some backup to keep order outside her court-room, then turned to Mary Alice.

"I want the transcript of the Grayson proceedings."

"I'm sure Judge Orr has already ordered it, Commissioner, but I'll make sure you get a copy."

Rei dumped her purse and briefcase on the small couch and began to pace. "I want mine as soon as possible. I need to see—I have to be sure—"

Mary Alice stepped in front of her to get her full attention. "I've been in the system for a long time and worked for a lot of judges. You're never sure. You just trust your instincts and the law and make the best decision you can."

"Did I make the best decision? I can think of two dozen people, those boys and their families, who could argue otherwise."

"Everybody makes mistakes, Commissioner. But don't forget the good we do here as well, okay? Now, I'll let you have a few minutes to get yourself together, but after that you've got to take the bench. We're already behind schedule."

Mary Alice closed the door behind her, but Rei could still hear the chaos out in the halls. She walked over to the window and stared out; however, all she could see was Bruce Grayson. The way he'd hung his head, the tears that clouded his dark eyes, the terror she thought she'd seen in his twelve-year-old face.

Do you regret your decision, Commissioner?
Commissioner, do you feel responsible?
Hell, yes, she felt responsible. Didn't she always?

THE SAND she was usually able to shovel against the tide threatened to swamp her today.

The morning sped by, due in part to several re quests for postponement. Rei recognized the tactic as a way for lawyers to have their cases reassigned to other courtrooms. She also recognized her own inability to concentrate. She considered herself a good judge of character, but today she had to question every innocent expression and statement of regret.

When Mary Alice called the last case before lunch, Rei was more than ready for a break. She wasn't going to get one. Acid churned in her gut as she watched Assistant State's Attorney Frank Dowd step up to the prosecutor's table. Something flickered in his gaze, impertinence perhaps? Derision and disappointment, certainly. Rei looked away.

Instead she picked up the file and flipped through it unnecessarily. "Okay, next we have the case of Gabriel Russo with the charge of threatening. I see Mr. Dowd for the State. And the defense would be?"

"Lukas Simon, Your Honor." A short, curly haired man stood up and buttoned his suit jacket. "We're looking to have the matter dropped. The whole thing's been blown out of proportion."

Maybe it had; maybe it hadn't. But the school and local authorities took any threat of violence very seriously in light of the incidents at Columbine and in Redlake, Minnesota.

"You know I can't do that, Mr. Simon." Rei ignored Dowd's smug look. "I see here in the file that the State's charges are based on a Web site—"

"Actually, posts to a Web log called *Out The Airlock*," Frank Dowd corrected.

"Thank you, blog entries as well as a handwritten list of fellow students."

"Yes, Your Honor. The State intends to prove that Gabriel Russo published threats against the people on his hit list—"

"Objection!" Lukas Simon then stood and addressed the prosecutor. "A hit list? Come on, Frank. For all the State knows, those are the people invited to Gabriel's next birthday party."

"I'd hate to find out what kind of party favors they'll be getting," Dowd retorted.

Rei glanced at the fourteen-year-old boy in question. He wore his jacket and tie uncomfortably and his dark-blond hair looked shaggy despite an attempt to tame it. He sat up straight with his hands folded before him on the table. The pallor of his face suggested nervousness, but she thought she saw anger in his deep brown eyes.

"This kid is a walking time bomb, Your Honor," Dowd continued. "When you combine the list with the threatening posts on the blog—"

"A combination the State never could have made if the principal hadn't broken into Gabe's locker!"

"*New Jersey v. T.L.O.*, Luke. The Supreme Court held that a locker is school property and school officials can conduct a search based on reasonable suspicion."

"I'm still trying to figure out the reasonable suspicion part, since Gabe isn't the only student who vents on that site. If it were a crime to mouth off about school bullies and social cliques, every kid between eleven and seventeen would be in a court-room," the defense lawyer countered.

Rei lightly tapped her gavel. "Let's calm down, people."

Frank Dowd stared at her, his gaze intent. "The State feels that the statements along with the list were sufficient to bring the charge. We have evidence of Gabriel Russo's anti-social behavior and plan to call witnesses who will attest to his volatile nature."

Rei looked over at the boy again and thought about Judge Orr's zero-tolerance directive. This case would be tough, one she might have relished any other time. But not today, not after the mistake she made with Bruce Grayson.

"All right, gentlemen, given the gravity of the ac-cusation, I'll hear witness testimony Wednesday morning. We're adjourned."

"CHRIS, COME HERE for a second."

Lara waved him over to the bar, her attention on the TV set mounted on the wall. When he was close enough for her to lower her voice, she nodded her head at the screen. "Hang on. This commercial is almost over."

He looked up to see the return of a midday news program—and Rei's pale, angry face pictured in a small window behind the anchorman's head.

"Isn't that one of our clients?" Lara asked.

"Yeah, it is. Turn it up, will you?" Chris listened to the newscaster recap the feature story. Apparently Rei's decision not to try this Grayson kid as an adult was being blamed for the uprising at the juvenile detention center.

His heart went out to her as he watched the footage of her fighting her way through a crowd of reporters. Despite the throng of people around her, she looked isolated. Her pale face was set in a calm mask, but, behind her glasses, her eyes shone with tears. He heard her voice crack as she murmured "no comment" for the fifth time.

"Lara, can you reschedule my appointments? I'm taking the rest of the day off."

She agreed and Chris thanked her, walking out of the bar past several clients, including Grant Bronson. Digging his cell phone out of his pocket, Chris dialed Rei's number as he continued out of the building.

"Yes?"

"You sound awful, sweetheart."

That got a watery laugh from her. "Thanks, Chris, that's just what I needed to hear."

"Where are you now?"

She sighed heavily into the phone. "The courthouse is a circus, so at the supervising judge's strong recommendation, I've cleared my docket for the rest of the day."

He reached for the keys to his pickup truck. "Okay, give me your address and I'll be at your place in an hour or so."

She gave him the address. "But you don't have to do that, Chris—"

"I'm doing it anyway. See you soon."

When Rei opened the door forty-five minutes later, she was wearing a silk blouse and tweed skirt but no shoes. He shifted the large shopping bag and bent down to give her a strong embrace and a kiss of reassurance. Then he moved around her to the living room. He heard her close the door and follow him as he set down the bag and took off his jacket.

"What's all this?"

"A little afternoon delight." He began to spread out a floral tablecloth on the carpet.

She groaned. "That old song? My clerk listens to the oldies station and they play it all the time."

"It's not the lyrics so much as the sentiment." He handed her the bouquet of a dozen peach roses from the bag. "If you'll put these in water and get us some plates, I've brought a bottle of the Chardonnay you liked, take-out from the chef at Lunch Meetings and chocolate-dipped strawberries. Everything I could think of to make you forget about your morning."

Rei hugged the roses to her with one arm and reached to cup his cheek with the other hand. She pulled him down for a tender kiss that nevertheless made him hot for her. She just seemed to affect him that way, equal parts lust and…

Love? Was that what he felt? A ribbon of anxiety skittered through his chest. It couldn't be, but then how would he know? Sure, he liked Rei a lot and enjoyed being with her. And he experienced an unusual sense of fulfillment when she was around. But love was something he created for others; he made it happen. It didn't happen to him. Chris deepened the kiss, concentrating on the lust part.

When Rei came up for air, he was glad to see a little smile on her face. "Careful, mister. I could get used to this."

"I could get used to doing it."

He hadn't realized how much until this moment. When he'd seen the news, all he could think about was getting to her, being there for her. Considering her aversion to commitment, he sure wasn't going to mention it to her yet. He'd just leave it alone and let things progress naturally.

Rei came back from the kitchen balancing plates and cutlery, two wine glasses and a corkscrew. "I didn't say it before, but thank you. This is a lovely surprise."

Chris waited until she sat down and he'd poured her wine. "Unlike the surprise this morning. Do you want to tell me what happened?"

"I apparently screwed up, that's what happened." Her mouth twisted into a scowl.

"Are you sure? Maybe you just missed something." He spooned cold prawns, steamed asparagus and portobello mushrooms next to the marinated bowtie pasta.

Rei made a face as she accepted the plate. "That makes me feel a lot better, knowing a twelve-year-old kid tugged on my heartstrings and played me like a concerto."

He swallowed a sip of the wine. "Sorry."

"Let's talk about something else, anything else." She took a bite of her pasta. "Like how good this food is."

"Okay, keep in mind that the public has an incredibly short attention span, and by tomorrow, this will fade from the media and some other story will have taken its place."

"Here's hoping." She raised her glass and took a sip. "So tell me about your day."

Chris helped himself to more of the shrimp. "Well, I might be getting a little ahead of myself, but I went looking at some commercial properties today. I think I found a place in Oakland that would be a great location."

"Oh, did you get the venture capital approved already?"

He shook his head. "Not yet, but it's only a matter of time, don't you think?"

Rei gave him an odd look and set her plate aside. "Why ask me? I have no influence over your funding."

"Why not you? You've seen firsthand how well Lunch Meetings is doing." Chris put his plate on top of hers and moved them both off the blanket. "In fact, I'd say you've gotten the best service I have to offer."

"Yes, I have, haven't I?"

"Are you doubting me?" There was a hint of reservation in her voice, so he leaned over to kiss her, nibbling her lips until they parted for him. "If you're unsatisfied, ma'am, I'd be happy to give you some extra special attention to make up for it."

She kissed him back and he felt her relax against him. "I'm definitely not satisfied. What are you going to do about it?"

Chris scooped his hand under her sweet little bottom and lifted her onto his lap. "There's only one thing to do in a situation like this…make love to you until you're persuaded of how good I am."

Her hands settled on his shoulders, then wrapped behind his neck. The heat of her skin burned through the thin material of his shirt. He stiffened when he felt the hot slide of her tongue along his earlobe. "Convince me."

Chris reached up to take off the barrette she wore and release the thick fall of her hair. As it tumbled down her back, he cupped the nape of her neck and sought her mouth again. With the tips of his tongue, he traced the contours of her lips and then coaxed them open. He kissed her more slowly, more tenderly, but with no less passion.

He slid his tongue along hers, tasting and savoring the sweetness of her, while his hands moved to undo the buttons of her blouse. He skimmed his hands up her smooth belly to cup her lace-covered breasts. Then he unhooked the front of the garment and pushed it off her shoulders along with her blouse.

Meanwhile, she had slipped her hands between them to unbutton his shirt. Now they stood together, bare torsos touching, hands caressing increasingly hot skin. The peaks of her nipples rubbed against his ribs as he tugged open the hook at the back of her skirt.

She cupped his erection through his clothes, drawing her thumb along his length before moving to unzip his trousers. They parted only long enough to remove the last of their clothing then together sank to the floor. Rei wrapped her arms about his neck and pulled him close for another kiss. He eased her back onto the smooth linen tablecloth before covering her body with his own.

Her naked breasts and all her smooth bare skin seared him, wreaking havoc with his senses. Chris indulged himself in the pleasure of touching her. His hands skimmed over her flawless skin, caressing the toned and sleek muscle, rediscovering the places that were susceptible to certain kinds of fondling. His mouth followed the path his hands had set and she quivered in response to his attentions.

Rei didn't utter a word as she stirred restlessly beneath him, rocking her hips in subtle encouragement. Her body told him in the language as old as time how much she wanted him. Heat, slow and molten, spread through him as he breathed in the scent of her desire.

Chris trailed a line of kisses along her throat and over her chest. He slid lower until her full breasts were accessible for his pleasure. Her hands sought his back, caressing his skin and massaging the muscle below the surface, as he rained kisses onto the velvet-soft orbs.

Taking one hard, straining nipple into his mouth, he suckled it to a sensitive peak. His tongue drew lazy swirls around the crest before turning his head to give its mate the same consideration. When his teeth gently scraped her ultraresponsive flesh, she squealed in unabashed ecstasy.

Then he shifted his weight to free his right arm. Chris reached among the silken curls between her thighs to find her soft feminine folds. Rei moaned softly and clutched at his shoulder while he rubbed her swollen clitoris in languid circles. She arched her hips against his hand as he slid his fingers in and out of her damp passage.

After reaching into his pants pocket, he made sure they were protected. Then he moved back over her, his body humming with need as he claimed her mouth. She nibbled his bottom lip before thrusting her tongue inside to taste and tease and tantalize. Rei spread her thighs, urging him to claim her completely.

She pressed her mouth to his throat, her hands gripping the hard muscles of his back, while he pushed into her wet passage, inch by inch, drawing out the moment of joining. Incredible emotion and fierce desire combined to intensify the sensation, but he struggled for control.

Her liquid heat enveloped the full length of him before he drew back a little at a time. He built the tension and anticipation, heightening the pleasure while prolonging the climax. Rei wiggled and strained beneath him, urging him on.

He slipped his palms under her hips, pulling her closer still. The need to be part of her drove him deeper, rocking him to the core. Unable to hold back any longer, he began thrusting heavily and she lifted her body to meet him. He felt the change inside her, felt her tighten around him. He cried out his release as she moaned his name.

Rei's breath fanned his neck as they held each other. Waiting for his pulse rate to slow, her body still joined with his, Chris felt a sense of belonging, of union. After a moment, he shifted his weight and they lay together, as close as possible without becoming one. It felt wonderful. It felt right.

He closed his eyes, feeling relaxed and yet tense at the same time. He stroked his fingers along the damp tendrils sticking to her temple and took a deep breath. There were things he wanted to say. But before he could, there were things he needed to hear, and so the words wouldn't come… And then the opportunity was lost when Rei turned her head to kiss his shoulder and sat up, rubbing her arms.

"It's chilly in here." She gathered her work clothes into a bundle. "I'll set the thermostat higher on my way to the ensuite."

"Sure. I'll clean up in here."

Chris washed in the downstairs powder room and got dressed. Then he went back into the living room to see to the picnic. Rei joined him in the kitchen a few moments later, now wearing a turtleneck and jeans.

As she passed by the phone, she stopped to press a button on the answering machine. "Five messages. I hope they're not from reporters."

"You don't have to respond if they are. That's what the delete button is for."

"Too bad you can't delete them in real life."

The first two calls were from telemarketers. He ignored them while Rei repackaged the leftover food and he put the plates into the dishwasher. When she bent over to get a storage container from one of the cabinet drawers, he ogled the snug fit of her jeans. He was surprised that his body responded so soon after they'd made love.

She straightened up, caught his admiring glance and grinned. "Don't you ever think about anything other than sex?"

"No, not when you're around." He rinsed out the sink and ran the disposal.

Rei, it's Dr. Solís. I've been trying to reach you all day. Please call me. You have got to reschedule those blood tests as soon as possible. I understand what you're afraid of, but you've put this off long enough. I hope to hear from you soon.

There was no mistaking the urgency he heard in the doctor's voice. Chris frowned and crossed the kitchen to Rei's side, reaching for her hand. Blood tests? His first thought was to wonder if she might be pregnant.

"What is it? What's wrong?" he asked.

"Reality has caught up with me." She didn't look at him, just kept staring at the floor.

Chris squeezed her icy fingers, not understanding, or rather, not wanting to. Slivers of fear crept through his veins. His body recognized what his mind refused to. "Rei?"

Finally she looked up at him. Her dark eyes had the glassy sheen of tears. When she spoke, her soft voice was breathy and strained. "You've never asked about my scar."

He shrugged, barely keeping his voice steady with a calm he didn't feel. "I have scars you never asked about, too."

"Mine is from surgery, a lumpectomy I had last year. I had breast cancer and—" Her voice broke. "It looks like it might be back."

No. Shock froze his next heartbeat. No...

Chris's numb fingers dropped her hand and he shook his head, refusing to believe what he'd heard. This couldn't be happening. He stepped back, his eyes racing over her body, looking for he had no idea what. It couldn't be true. She looked fine.

She had to be fine.

"I...I don't know. What can I say?" He continued to stare at her in some crazy attempt to convince himself it wasn't true.

"There's nothing else you need to say."

Her voice sounded oddly harsh. His gaze returned to her face and he saw the anguish, the utter bewilderment and anger, and knew it was true. Rei had cancer.

Pain stabbed into the hollow void in his chest

that he'd thought might finally be filled. They had only just found each other. He'd only just acknowledged how much he cared for her. He hadn't even told her yet. And now... Chris released the breath he was holding.

"You'll be fine," he whispered, and fought to control his panic. He had to be strong. But icy fear was twisting around his heart. *Don't leave me. Don't leave.* And yet he should have known. Didn't everyone he cared about abandon him eventually? "You're going to be fine, Rei. You'll be just fine."

Don't think about it. Don't let it hurt....

REI FELT HER heart twist and bleed inside her chest. If Chris told her she'd be fine in that patronizing voice one more time, she'd hit him.

She stared at the expression of revulsion and rejection on his face, and let anger flare to the surface. She'd opened herself up, allowed herself to trust him. Now when she needed comfort and support, he backed away from her like she'd grown a second head.

"I'd like you to go now, Chris."

"You shouldn't be by yourself right now."

Like being with him while her heart shattered into a thousand pieces was better? Her misery was like a physical pain, so she once again tapped into her anger. He'd advised her not to paint every man with the same brush, then showed his true colors to be just like her ex-boyfriend Jake's, just like her father's.

She could handle being discarded. She'd done it

before. "You don't have to stay. I'll be fine. In fact, I don't need you, Chris. I don't want you."

He looked lost for words but she ignored his false concern and swept past him. He reached for her, but she yanked her arm away. In the foyer, she felt bitter anguish rising in her chest, choking her, and she fought against the tears. Not now. Not in front of him. She ran up the stairs, locking herself in the bedroom.

"Rei?"

He'd followed her, knocking softly on the door while she threw herself onto the bed. She turned her head so the pillows muffled her sobs.

"Rei? Will you let me in?"

Her answer was silence. She'd already done that and look what had happened. Wrapping the down comforter more securely around her shoulders, she curled deeper into the sheets. She'd turned up the thermostat but couldn't get warm. The cold was too deep inside of her.

11

Tuesday, April 22nd

Accomplishments: Face something you fear

"THANKS FOR COMING with me, P.J."

"You're only thanking me because you know I'm furious with you." She slouched down in the waiting room chair and crossed her arms. "I would have come with you sooner if you'd bothered to tell me. That's what best friend means, honey. I'm going to kick your butt as soon as the doctor tells us you're fine."

There was that word again.

Rei nodded at the linoleum floor tiles of the diagnostic imaging waiting room, using her left hand to hold a gauze pad against her other elbow. She hated having blood drawn at the best of times. There was the awful prick of metal through skin and the creepy feeling of the needle inside her vein and, worst of all, at her age there was no lollipop for being a good girl.

She lifted the gauze to see if the puncture was healing yet, then pressed it back down. Another minute. She did have another minute, right? Oh brother, she hoped so. She'd taken off her watch last night, or was it early this morning, because she didn't want to see the time ticking away from her.

"I'm scared, Peej."

"I'm not." She spoke with a bright confidence that belied the dark shadows under her eyes. "There's absolutely nothing to worry about."

Rei lifted the corner of her mouth but failed to smile. Chris had said the same thing, but his closed expression had been the polar opposite of her best friend's bravado. "Why? Because you said so?"

"That's right." P.J. leaned over and took her hand. "I'm the Queen of the World. And as Ruler of the Planet, I'm not about to let you have cancer again. There's no way you're going to be anything but healthy. No way."

The tears Rei had been trying to control slipped over her lashes and down her cheeks as P.J. pressed a kiss to her forehead and sniffled. Pressure was building inside of her, and she just wanted to scream and scream. Instead she swallowed hard against the lump in her throat, wiped peach lipstick off her temple and took a deep breath.

"What you are, Phoebe Jayne, is a lunatic. I'm already Supreme Overlord of the Universe, so the planet falls under my jurisdiction."

"No way! If you were Supreme Overlord, chocolate would have zero fat content and the 49ers would have won a Super Bowl by now." P.J. gave a muffled laugh.

A tiny bubble of amusement formed in her chest,

pushing a little of her fear aside. Rei wiped her eyes and grinned. "Yeah, we'd be trim but never have to exercise, and it would be impossible to have wrinkles and zits at the same time."

"Rei Davis?" A nurse stood in the doorway, smiling vaguely and holding a sheaf of papers. "We're ready for you."

After squeezing P.J.'s hand, she followed the nurse into the dressing area. She stripped off everything from the waist up then slipped a thin paper gown over the goosebumps forming on her arms. With a sense of inevitability, she walked into the imaging room feeling chilled from more than the arctic temperature that protected the machines.

Her heart thundered in her chest. Rei took a deep breath and lifted her arm behind her head. The technician flattened her breast onto the X-ray machine and lowered the top plate.

Please, God. Please…

TWENTY MINUTES after the test, Rei was back in the waiting area. Waiting.

She felt nauseated but hadn't been able to eat so much as a piece of dry toast this morning. Acid churned in her stomach while she tried to prepare herself for whatever the X-ray films might show. Apprehension shot through her like bolts of lightning, striking her temples, neck and lower back.

She'd been so lucky last year. What were the chances that her luck would hold?

"Ms. Davis?"

The nurse stood before her and it took all Rei's willpower to look up from the woman's white sneakered feet to see her face. Her smiling face.

"Ms. Davis, the films came back clear. We'll send the results to Dr. Solís, but everything looks good. You're free to go home anytime."

P.J. wrapped her in a huge hug and squealed. "Oh, I'm so relieved!"

Everything looked good. Rei closed her eyes and sagged against P.J.'s shoulder. Now that some of the weight was lifted, core-deep weariness set in. She had part of the answer she longed to hear. Everything looked good.

"I didn't want you to know how worried I was, but I was." P.J. squeezed her harder, then rubbed a hand over her back. "But now you're okay for sure!"

Rei gently extricated herself from the embrace and shook her head. "The *mammogram* is negative. That means there's no evidence the cancer has recurred in either of my breasts."

"I know! This is great—"

"But I still have to wait for the blood test results." She spoke quietly from relief, fatigue and continued concern.

P.J. cocked her head and frowned. "I don't understand. You don't have breast cancer anymore. Do you?"

Rei sighed and gave an uncertain shrug. "If the CA 27.29 antigen shows up again, it would mean the cancer came back somewhere else."

PLEASE CALL ME
Sender has requested a read confirmation.
Send confirmation of receipt? Yes No
I have no idea what you're going through, Rei, but you don't have to go through it by yourself.
I left you alone last night like you asked. But today I want to hear your voice and hold you in my arms and find out what your doctor said.
The other e-mails I sent didn't seem to go through. Neither did my voice mails. Please call me when you get this message.
Chris

HE CLICKED the "send" button and minimized his e-mail program with an odd sense of finality.

He hadn't heard from Rei at all, not even an electronic receipt that the e-mail had been opened. He wanted to give her the benefit of the doubt that she'd been too upset to get on her computer last night. But, as much as he worried about her, he couldn't deny his resentment at being shut out. Again.

As her friend, he prayed that she was going to be all right. But, as her lover, they were finished. For each step he tried to take forward, she backpedaled three. He could still hear the message behind her last words to him. *I don't want you. I don't need you.*

Well, he didn't need the emotional confusion. Not on top of the anger and betrayal he was dealing with this morning.

Chris yanked the ringing phone off the hook. It had been a long, sleepless night and his nerves were frayed, leaving him feeling exposed and irritated.

Reaching up with both hands, he massaged the base of his neck. This could very well go down as one of the worst days of his life. From the minute he'd walked into his office, he'd been fielding phone calls from clients canceling their services. If he thought for one minute he could get away with it, Grant Bronson would already be a homicide statistic.

The son of a bitch had used their college acquaintance as leverage for gaining Chris's trust. He'd given Grant courtship counseling in good faith only to find out the bastard was a tabloid reporter working undercover. The story had run in the early edition of the Inquirer this morning and clients had been calling ever since.

He looked up at a knock on his office door. Lara stuck her head in, frown lines etched deeply into her forehead. "I've had six cancellations by phone, there are four people waiting in the lobby to talk to you in person and I haven't even looked at my e-mails yet."

"Okay, Lara. Find a temp agency and see if we can hire a receptionist to answer calls and take messages for the rest of the day. Hang on." Chris paused as his phone rang. "Hello?"

"Yeah, this is Bob Dawson. How come you never gave me any special treatment?"

"Mr. Dawson, I'm sorry—"

"I didn't get no private sessions and I didn't find a good match, either. I want a refund."

Chris reached up to massage his temples. "Someone from accounting will get back to you on that, Mr. Dawson. We'd appreciate your patience while we sort things out. Thank you." He hung up the phone, muttering, "Murder is too good for him."

Lara cocked her head. "Excuse me?"

"Sorry, I was thinking about Bronson. Can you also call our lawyers at Kensington and Style to find out if we have any recourse against the newspaper?"

"Sure, Chris. But I wouldn't hold out much hope." Lara closed the door behind her.

He didn't. In fact, he didn't have any hope. Not only wouldn't he be able to open new locations, he'd be lucky to keep this one open.

"FALSE POSITIVE. Is that some kind of oxymoron?" P.J. lifted her hand to get the waiter's attention.

"It means you owe me a butt kicking, thank God." Rei smiled. She was almost lightheaded with relief and a kind of giddy euphoria coursed through her, like the warm afterglow of a fine wine.

The waiter at Café Stefani refilled their glasses and cleared away the appetizer plates.

"Dr. Solís explained that sometimes other conditions can indicate cancer where there isn't actually a recurrence. In my case, I suffer with endometriosis and that may have caused the incorrect test result."

P.J. raised her tea glass. "Here's to mistakes, honey."

Despite the overcast sky and cool temperatures, Rei had insisted that they eat lunch outside. She wanted to feel the teasing hint of spring in the air, let the light breeze touch her face and just breathe. She was having trouble adjusting mentally. Having been so afraid she might be sick again, she couldn't quite believe that she'd dodged that bullet.

When her cell phone rang, she picked it up to check the caller display. 415-555-4681, Chris's number. She let it ring again. What was he calling her for? Wait, that wasn't fair. He was a decent guy.

But while part of her wanted to hear his voice, the rest of her was too tired for more intense emotions. She hadn't realized how worried she'd really been, despite her efforts at denial, and the stress had taken its toll.

P.J. speculated, "A frantic call from Mary Alice asking you to come into court?"

"It's Chris."

"I'll bet he's pretty frantic, too, now that everybody knows he's some kind of con artist."

Rei frowned and shook her head. "What do you mean?"

"Sorry. Of course you've been preoccupied." P.J. pulled what looked like a tabloid newspaper from her tote bag and slid it across the table. "The Board is foaming at the mouth over my poor investment choice. It looks like Lunch Meetings won't be getting the expansion loan after all."

Rei reached for the copy of the *San Francisco*

Inquirer and read the banner, her curiosity rapidly transforming to dismay with each word.

Dating Service Setup!
Lunch Meetings Matchmaker Pulls Strings Behind the Scenes

Printed beneath the headline was a small headshot of Chris, as well as one of him kissing Rei on the front step of her house. The article started off with a general description of the dating service, but quickly segued into a behind-the-scenes recap that included quotes from several Lunch Meetings clients.

The reporter even went so far as to wonder if "Mr. London's girlfriend, Rei Davis, a Superior Court Commissioner and daughter of esteemed Associate Justice Gordon Davis, knew about his date doctor scheme and shared his disregard for propriety. Readers may recall that Commissioner Davis was recently in the news for awarding a light sentence to a violent gang member."

The story told of Chris's efforts to affect clients' behavior modification from clothes shopping and etiquette lessons, to trips to local nightclubs and prearranged dates. Rei immediately thought about the night at Divas. Chris had told her he'd been there with a client. She'd thought it was a coincidence, their meeting at the club, but what if he'd somehow followed P.J.?

Her friend had accused him of a setup. Could P.J. be right?

Her thoughts turned to their conversation in the Zuni Café. When she'd accused him of stealing information and betraying her trust, he'd denied it. There was no way she would return his call now. How could she ever trust him again?

"Looks like we ended it just in time." She tossed the newspaper onto the table and reached for her tea.

P.J. gave her hand a sympathetic squeeze. "Oh, Rei. What happened?"

She closed her eyes, turning her face toward the pale sunlight. But, unable to escape the memory of Chris's expression and the hurt that expression caused, she opened them again.

"I made the mistake of letting down my guard, of thinking long term." She told P.J. about the night she'd gotten Dr. Solís's call. "I didn't date a lawyer, but the ending was the same."

P.J. regarded her with wise, blue eyes. "Not quite. I think you really fell for this guy."

"Maybe. Maybe I did. But I'll get over it." She shrugged. Even as she said it, though, Rei recognized the fact that Chris wasn't like the other men she'd dated. She really had let herself care this time.

"I'm sorry, for your sake, that it's over."

"Hey, it's for the best, right? I'm glad I found out now, instead after the 'in sickness and in health' part of the vows."

P.J. ignored her attempt at a joke. "Talk to Chris. There's probably a logical explanation for all of this, and you two might be able to work it out."

"I don't think so, Peej. No matter what he says, I can't forget that instinctive first reaction." Rei looked down at the sticky medical tape residue inside her right elbow. "It hurts less if you rip a bandage off quickly."

P.J. tilted her head and nibbled her lower lip, a habit that signified there was something on her mind. Rei knew from experience just to wait it out, and indeed P.J. finally drew a breath and haltingly began to speak.

"You know, we've known each other for a long time. And I sometimes wonder how our friendship has lasted this long. You are bright and witty and loyal and so many other good things. But, Rei, you're also one of the least forgiving people I've ever met."

She gasped, stunned by the blunt observation and by the cold recognition of truth. For what seemed like the hundredth time in the past twenty-four hours, tears stung the back of her eyes. Rei felt too dejected to even get angry.

"I'm sorry, Rei, but it's true. The instant someone disappoints you, you cut them out of your life."

She realized what P.J. had said was true and cringed inside. Rei drew patterns in the condensation on her glass, not meeting P.J.'s eye. "You make me sound like a complete bitch."

"You're not a bitch. You're a woman whose protective shell has grown into plated armor. Outside of the courtroom, you never give anyone a second chance. That makes it harder for them to hurt you, but you never give them an opportunity to make up for it either."

Was this the reason the men in her life were never around when she needed them, why it was so hard for her to make close friends? Had she subconsciously done something to push them away? She thought back over several relationships, about offences big and small. She wasn't wrong. Those people had let her down. Hadn't they?

Rei shifted uncomfortably in her seat. She was getting psychoanalyzed every time she turned around lately. "So what's your advice? Call Chris and restart a relationship that was founded on deception?"

P.J.'s intense gaze contradicted her gentle tone. "Chris isn't the man you need to talk to, honey. You'll never get any sense of closure until you resolve your issues with Gordon."

Rei felt her expression harden along with her voice. "Yeah, like that's going to happen."

"Then you need to accept the fact that you're never going to be whole or happy."

REI SPENT most of Saturday in bed. She'd earned a day of wallowing in self-pity, something she normally didn't indulge in. But, frankly, it had been a hellacious week and all she wanted to do was sleep. Sleep was the ultimate avoidance tactic—except when it resulted in dreams.

She stood on the edge of a canyon, a frigid wind howling in her ears and slapping against her face. There were people all around her—friends, acquaintances and coworkers, family.

She tried to speak but no one seemed to hear her. Then she realized she was encased in a bubble of glass.

Though she stood among the crowd, she couldn't touch them and they couldn't get through to her. They reached out for her, but she slipped over the precipice, falling into isolated darkness.

Rei awoke with a start, her heart racing and the stale residue of nightmares clinging to her skin. Her temples throbbed with a slight headache. Shoving the covers aside, she got up and padded to the en suite where she ran warm water over a cloth. After washing her face, she looked up and caught sight of herself in the mirror.

Usually when she looked, she noticed only the sum of her parts, not her face as a whole. Had she always appeared this stern? Did her eyes always look so uncompromising?

Was this how people saw her?

P.J. had held up a different kind of mirror today, and she'd liked her reflection in that one even less. It hurt to be accused of sharing the fault for her failed relationships. She'd thought she had changed, but maybe she hadn't come as far from her pre-cancer days as she claimed. Rei turned aside and left the bedroom.

After half-heartedly slapping a sandwich together in the kitchen, Rei wandered back upstairs to the office, still in her nightshirt in the middle of the day. She turned on the computer with the intention of checking the news. The best way to stop feeling sorry for herself was to remember that others had it so much worse.

Her e-mail program opened before the Internet browser, though. There were five messages from Chris each successively shorter until she reached this last:

HOW ARE YOU?
I know we're through, but what did the doctor say? Are you all right?
Chris

We're through.
She had spoken the words earlier today, the words that she should have anticipated hearing from him. She had no right to feel surprised or sad or disappointed, and yet her sense of loss went beyond tears. Chris was so much more than a great lover. He was charming and sweet and patient, more patient than she deserved maybe.

Having never reached out before, where did she begin? Begin with the obvious. But what did she want to say? She missed him, missed his affection and friendship. But, despite taking P.J.'s words to heart, she believed she had grounds for not fully trusting Chris.

And where did that leave them? Nowhere really.

RE: HOW ARE YOU?
I'm okay. Thanks for asking.
Rei

HE'D FINALLY heard from Rei and her reply couldn't have been colder. He didn't know if she meant she wasn't sick, or if she was just blowing him off. He hoped it was the former and he wished her well. But, even though he missed her and worried about her, he was through chasing after someone who didn't want to get caught.

Chris frowned as he pulled his truck in front of his mother's house. There was a blue Toyota Camry parked next to her Honda in the driveway. He recognized it in abstract disbelief, but a quick check of the tag number confirmed that it was his father's car.

What the hell was he doing here?

He opened the front door and walked through the foyer toward the back of the house. "Hello? Mom?"

"In the living room, dear."

Sunlight streamed through the glass sliders, illuminating the tableau. Chris faltered in mid-stride at the sight of his parents sitting, side by side, on the green striped couch. It wasn't their proximity after so long that shocked him as much as their relaxed demeanor. They appeared as if it were perfectly normal for them to be sharing a seat, when to his knowledge, they hadn't spoken in years.

"Hello, son." His father looked at him warily and shifted away, widening the space between him and Jeanna.

But his mother reached for his hand and greeted Chris with a quiet smile. "Hi, sweetheart. I was expecting you to stop by today."

"What's going on, Mom?"

"Come and sit down, Chris."

He walked further into the room and chose an armchair across from his parents, who were holding hands. He felt like he was in the Twilight Zone, seeing but not quite believing.

Jeanna took a deep breath and glanced at David. She exhaled with a little laugh. "I don't know how to tell you this. I realize it's a bit of a shock. But your father is the man I've been dating. He and I are getting back together."

She waited for his reaction with an expression of pleased anticipation. Chris looked at his father for confirmation, then back at Jeanna. "Why?"

His mother startled and the happy glow faded slightly from her face. The question had been spoken more harshly than he'd intended. But he couldn't help the sudden flood of anger, false hope and resentment that filled him.

David faced him directly and calmly held his accusatory gaze. "I understand this may be difficult for you and your sisters to understand, Chris. I did wrong by your mother, and by you kids, and you have no idea how sorry I am."

"No, Dad, I guess I don't. What do you think, that you're just going to pick up where you left off? With the emphasis on being on the word *left.*"

He knew he was being unfair, but Chris couldn't seem to help himself. On the one hand, he was glad for the gleam in his mother's eyes, for the bright color in her cheeks. But the angry, abandoned boy inside him demanded to know how David dared try to come back into their lives like this.

"I'm the luckiest man in the world that your mother is willing to try again. We've talked a lot over the past months and I've tried to make it up to her. She's the only woman I've ever loved and I'm going to do my damnedest to make her happy. I know it's a lot to ask, but I'm hoping we might be a real family again."

This was what he'd longed for as a boy, but as a grown man who had too often faced disappointment, Chris found himself less than forgiving. "What happens if it doesn't work out, Mom? What if things get tough or even just uncomfortable? How can you trust him not to walk out again?"

He and his father had never really dealt with this, never talked about what David had done or how Chris felt about it. They had ignored the wall between them, talked around it, stepping aside and pretending it wasn't there while it grew taller and thicker.

His mother's gaze softened, her hazel eyes sympathetic but determined. "Sometimes, my darling, you have to have faith. You have to trust people to do the right thing. I believe your father has changed and is deserving of a second chance."

"Looking back, it all made sense at the time. But it's so hard to explain now." David hung his head and sighed. "We married young and I guess I had this illusion of what my life would be like. When our marriage didn't meet those impossible expectations, we drifted apart until the gulf seemed too wide to cross. So

I walked away from the best thing that ever happened to me, searching in vain for something better."

Chris scoffed. It had been a lame-assed excuse the first time he'd heard it and it didn't sound any better now. "Did you find it, Dad? Did you find something worth hurting everyone you claimed to love?"

His father looked up and shook his head. "No, son, I didn't. It was the biggest mistake I've ever made, but I didn't realize until it was too late."

"But it's not too late for us, Chris. It's never really too late if you can find forgiveness in your heart." Jeanna's tone of voice begged him to unbend, to meet his father halfway. "Life is spanned by small bridges between people and those bridges have to go in both directions."

David kissed Jeanna's temple then got up from the couch. He walked over and stood in front of Chris, looking down at him but not down on him. "A man has to admit when he's made a huge mistake and be brave enough to ask for that second chance. I'm blessed that your mother has forgiven me. I don't expect you to. But I'm asking anyway." He put out his hand.

The last time he'd cried had been the day his father left. Now, on the day his father was asking to come back, Chris felt tears sting his eyes for the first time in nineteen years. He felt a tightness in his chest and reminded himself to breathe. In his mind, he saw the wall begin to crumble, a few bricks at a time. It was time to rebuild it as a bridge.

Chris stood slowly, unable to resist the pleading

in David's gaze and took the offered hand. "Welcome home, Dad."

The tears he'd been holding back appeared in his father's eyes. David squeezed his hand once then dropped it to take his son in his arms for a long overdue embrace.

12

AS HE WALKED toward courtroom number 420, Chris noticed the smell of industrial strength pine cleaner. It couldn't quite mask the odor of desperation wafting through the air. His greeting encompassed the whole family, apprehensively waiting in the hallway, but Chris's focus was on his nephew.

"Hey, G-man. How're you doing?"

"How do you think?"

Gabe delivered the reply in the surliest voice possible but Chris saw the fear in the boy's eyes and ignored it. He sat down on the hard bench and draped an arm over Gabe's shoulder. "It's going to be okay."

"This is totally bogus, Uncle Chris." He wiped a hand over his face. "Okay, yeah, I got mad about some guys who were messing with me. But I was never going to hurt any of them."

"I know it's hard to believe it right now, but you'll get through this. You've got your whole family behind you."

Chris looked up at Diana and Michael who were talking with Luke Simon, the attorney they'd hired.

He wasn't sure whether his sister and her husband would be able to work out all of their differences, but judging by the way Michael rested his hand on Di's waist, they were at least going to stand together for their son's sake.

He shifted his gaze to his parents. David and Jeanna sat on the next bench with his sister Andrea, waiting for Gabriel's case to be called. He still couldn't get over the sight of them holding hands. A pleasant glow warmed his heart. He'd been waiting a long time for this and hoped that this time really was until death did they part.

Chris adjusted his necktie and smoothed it over his shirt. They were all here to offer moral support, and if the judge allowed it, to act as character witnesses. Gabriel's immediate and possibly his long-term future was on the line, so it was important that he make a good impression in the courtroom.

However, if Chris were honest with himself, the choice to wear his best suit and favorite tie was in hopes of running into Rei. He'd thought about calling her on the pretext of asking her advice on Gabe's behalf, but then told himself he wasn't going to chase her. She obviously didn't want him to.

Though just because their relationship was over didn't mean he'd stopped caring, wondering how she was and praying for her to be all right. He wasn't sure where to find her and he didn't want to wander the halls and miss Gabe's case being called. Maybe he'd try to locate her after this hearing.

If she was even here. Chris raked a hand over his hair. Hell, it hadn't occurred to him that she might have taken a leave of absence to begin whatever treatments her doctor had recommended. He'd done some Internet research and apparently chemotherapy often made the patient feel worse than the cancer itself.

"Gabriel Russo?"

His thoughts were interrupted and his heart gave a nervous leap when the bailiff called Gabe's name. Chris looked over to see the look of panic on his nephew's face. He patted Gabe's knee then stood as the lawyer came over to escort them into the courtroom.

Chris held the heavy wooden door for his mother and waited for his dad to precede him before following them inside. The courtroom was smaller than he'd imagined, so he wasn't halfway down the aisle before he saw the judge's face. Shadows darkened her eyes and her mouth was set in a firm line.

Rei looked tired and preoccupied, but he smiled anyway, glad to see her despite his resolve. She, however, did not seem at all happy to see him. Her brows drew together in surprise when she looked up from the papers she'd been studying. For a second, Chris thought he saw welcome in her gaze but it disappeared almost instantly.

"Mr. Simon, what is Mr. London doing here?"

Gabe's attorney shot him a puzzled look before addressing Rei. "He's the defendant's uncle, Your Honor. He's one of the witnesses I intend to call to—"

"Both counsel, approach the bench." Rei shot him

a quick glance, looking vaguely apologetic, before turning her attention to the lawyers.

"What's going on?" Gabe asked in confusion.

His mother touched his arm. "How in the world do you know the judge, Chris?"

He lowered his voice so no one beyond the family could overhear. "She's the woman I was dating until recently."

"Oh, you never told me about her." Jeanna looked over towards the judge's bench.

He looked at Rei as well, his chest tight with longing and regret. "There's nothing to tell."

CHRIS LOOKED wonderful. She'd never seen him in a suit before and the formality of it added a certain sexiness to his boyish good looks. The ripple of pleasure traveled from her heart to all the nerves in her body, finally settling between her thighs. The reaction annoyed and distracted her.

She *was* glad to see him, just not under these circumstances. "I'm not at liberty to speak with you. This isn't the time or place."

She glanced up and down the western corridor nearest the Administrator's office, where she'd just asked that Commissioner Whitney take over the Russo case. Rei sincerely hoped no one witnessed this ex parte conversation. If she was seen talking to Chris, she'd get her hat handed to her by the supervising judge. After the Grayson fiasco, she couldn't take that chance.

"Listen to me, Rei. Please."

His superior height and larger body blocked her escape from the alcove near the stairs. Chris wasn't threatening her and he couldn't possibly know it, but his posture reminded her of someone else who used physical intimidation to make a point.

"We have nothing to discuss, Chris."

When she started to move around him, he put out his arm in entreaty. "This isn't about us. It's about an angry and misunderstood boy who—"

"About whom I don't want to hear another word. I can't, okay?" She gripped the folds of her robe and tried to make him understand. "I am barred by the canon of ethics from discussing any of my cases, especially those involving a minor."

Chris's focus remained on her as his voice took on an earnest tone. "We've talked about Gabe before and you know he's basically a good kid. It's just that this divorce has got him upset and confused."

Rei looked up in time to see what she'd dreaded most. Judge Orr was coming down the hall. Now she found herself grateful for Chris's ability to overshadow her. "You're the one who seems to be confused. I recused myself from the case and postponed it for reassignment to avoid any suggestion of impropriety."

"If you're not going to hear the case anymore, there shouldn't be a problem."

"There's still a problem, though you obviously can't see it." As soon as the supervising judge had passed, she drew herself up to her full height and pleaded with him to appreciate the position she was in.

"I respect the zealous way you're defending your nephew, it's admirable. And I realize you're used to manipulating opportunities to get the result you want, but that is not going to happen in this matter, understand? It's out of my hands."

"I see you read the tabloids." Chris's eyes darkened with resignation and his mouth twisted into a smirk. "All I'm asking is for someone to listen, to see the truth and make the offer of another chance."

Were they talking about Gabe, or about their relationship? This was a test, a chance for her to prove that she wasn't judgmental. But damn it, the timing was all wrong. She reached out to briefly touch his hand and felt the same tingling energy as the first night they'd met. "We can talk later, okay? Right now I have to go."

When Chris turned, creating an exit route, Rei pulled the robe tighter around her and started to walk away. She was just about past him when he cleared his throat. "How are you? Are you…okay?"

She looked up to catch the worry in his gaze before the shutter came down and his expression became impersonal. No, she wasn't okay. She was angry and confused and disappointed and she missed him. There was a big empty space in her life where he was supposed to be.

"I'm fine, Chris. It was a false alarm. A second round of testing showed that the cancer is still in remission."

"I'm glad to hear that, Rei. Really." His shoulders

sagged a bit, releasing tension, and he gave her a little smile. He opened his mouth, as if there was something else on his mind, but then simply nodded.

She continued to hold his gaze, giving him the opportunity to say what he needed to. But the silence stretched on painfully and the gulf widened between them. She wanted to bridge it, though she wasn't sure how since nothing had been resolved, and she reached for him again.

"Chris—"

"You have to go, remember?" He looked away. "Take care of yourself."

She drew back her hand and sighed. "Yeah, you, too."

Chin down, Rei marched down the hall in the direction of her chambers. She was determined to keep it together until she could close the door and have a good cry, something she'd been doing a lot lately. She wouldn't have the chance, however. Someone stepped in front of her and she jerked her head up.

Associate Justice Gordon Davis frowned down at her. "What the hell were you thinking, Rei?"

HER CHAMBERS FELT too small with her father in it, especially when he invaded her personal space. Rei hid her reaction, though, and forced herself not to back down.

"You've embarrassed me, smearing the family name through the tabloids." He smacked the newspaper he held with the back of his other hand. "And, as if that weren't bad enough, I come to discuss your transgression only to find you carrying on with a witness."

"I turned the Russo case over to another judge as soon as I realized there was a conflict."

"That's something at least. You're never going to be taken seriously if you continue to exhibit such a lack of good sense and judgment."

As he continued his tirade, Rei simmered with resentment. He never listened to anything she said, except those portions he could use against her later. He hoarded her words and feelings like ammunition then shot her down when she least expected it.

"I was right to push you as hard as I did, though I don't know why I bothered. You've never lived up to your potential."

Rei looked at him, noting that once again a man was using his size to keep her in place. Chris was the same size as her father, as tall and as broad. He too had challenged her over Gabriel, but instead of intimidating her, he'd simply stood his ground and made his appeal.

In an instant of crystal clarity, she realized P.J. was right—she couldn't move forward as long as the past was holding her back. "No, Dad. I've never lived up to your *expectations* and that's not the same thing."

Gordon paused, highly displeased at the interruption. "Excuse me?"

Rei cleared her throat. "I've exceeded my potential. You'd know that if just once you'd see me for who I really am, not the way you want me to be."

Gordon scoffed. "If you could be what I wanted,

you certainly wouldn't be wasting your time in kiddie court."

"'Kiddie court' is the best job I've ever had, the most rewarding, the most important." Rei fanned the spark of anger to bolster her courage. "I'd rather suffer the consequences of the few Bruce Graysons than make the mistake of not showing leniency to the many Gabriel Russos. Believe it or not, Dad, I'm a damned good judge."

"Of course, you are. You're a Davis when you bother to remember it, and I wouldn't expect anything less."

He didn't get it. As usual, it was all about him. He was small-minded and small-hearted, needing to tear people down in order to make himself better.

"I doubt that you realize it, but you're the reason I fight so hard for the kids in my courtroom. I'm a good person. I'm smart and caring and have a lot of other positive traits. But you've never acknowledged them because it was easier to keep me in a box called inadequate."

He looked away from her steady gaze and moved back a step. "I never said that you're inadequate. But you do tend to make unwise choices—refusing the offer from Stanford, leaving your corporate law firm. Now you're involved with some kind of matchmaking con artist. This is not acceptable for a jurist and member of my family, Rei."

She smiled sadly, knowing he would never understand and that it was time for her to let go of her expectations as well. "We're not a family. Not since before

Mom died. We're just two people who were once forced by blood and circumstance to live together."

"How dare you? I raised you to show more respect." Gordon threw the newspaper to the floor at her feet.

Rei flinched but stood her ground. "You want respect but you've never given it in return."

It was as if she hadn't spoken. Gordon continued to scowl at her, his brown eyes boring into hers. "I demand an apology, young lady. Right now."

"I am sorry, Dad. I'm very sorry for all that should have been and may never be."

She could tell by the unyielding expression on his face, by the rejection in his eyes, that he wouldn't change and so neither would their relationship. In her heart a part of her would always want to be Daddy's precious girl, but she realized she'd never live up to his expectations and she no longer wanted to try.

This was her father's game and she didn't want to play anymore.

"I wanted so much for you to love me, Dad. But I can't remember a time you ever said it, and even if you had I wouldn't have believed you. Actions really do speak louder than words."

He stared at her, uncharacteristically speechless, and for a moment she thought that, for once, something had gotten through to him. Then without another word, he spun on his heel and walked stiffly toward the door.

Rei watched him go, her heart breaking a little more with each step. For most of her life she'd viewed her father as judgmental and intimidating and hurtful. But now, as if she were looking through a window after sweeping the curtains aside, she finally saw him clearly. Gordon was human, a sad, dysfunctional man who didn't know how to be a father. Realizing that, she felt liberated from the past.

Then suddenly he paused, the knob gripped tightly in his fist. He spoke without turning around.

"About Hunter's high school graduation."

Rei braced herself for the final rejection. She had stood up to him, challenged his authority and there was no way he would allow that loss of control. But that was okay; she'd said what she needed to and crossed over to healing.

"Yes?"

"I'll expect you—that is, you're welcome. Unless you have other plans."

Rei smiled and blinked away the haze of moisture from her eyes. "I'll be there."

Wednesday, April 23rd

Accomplishments: Make peace with the past;
Admit when you're wrong

JadeBlossom is now online
JadeBlossom is instant messaging you

JadeBlossom: I did it.

PajamaPartyGirl: Did what?

JadeBlossom: I called my father a selfish, self-centered arrogant jerk.

PajamaPartyGirl: YOU WHAT????

JadeBlossom: Okay, maybe I didn't use those exact words. But I did it, P.J. I finally stood up to him and told him how much he's hurt me. I still can't believe it. I was so hesitant to confront him. But I did it.

PajamaPartyGirl: I'm so proud of you! You turned the light on the monster in the closet and saw how small a shadow he casts.

JadeBlossom: Yes, the monster was only a man after all. It's funny, I see parents like him all the time in court but never recognized Gordon for the bully he is. And like most bullies, he backed down when he realized I wasn't going to let him intimidate me anymore.

PajamaPartyGirl: That's great! You must feel so good.

JadeBlossom: I don't know how I feel. I thought there would be some kind of epiphany, some magic moment that shouted, "The past is over!"

PajamaPartyGirl: There won't be one moment but a series of them. It took years for this pain to build,

so you can't expect it to ease with a single conversation. Give yourself some time. You had the
strength to face him. You have the power to let go
and you now have the freedom to make better
choices in your relationships.

JadeBlossom: I don't even know where to begin.

PajamaPartyGirl: Call Chris.

THURSDAY NIGHT after work, Rei slowly turned the
pages of her Life List journal, looking over the items
she'd written there. Though she'd managed to check
off several more goals, there was still so much she
wanted to do.

Twice now she'd been blessed with the gift of life,
and although she'd untied the ribbon and torn off the
wrapping paper, she had yet to open the box and
truly appreciate what was inside. It was time for her
to look beyond the moment, to believe in the future
and live as though she had one.

It was time for her to take the greatest risk of all.

Rei picked up the phone and dialed Chris's home
number. When the digital answering machine picked
up, she started to speak and then changed her mind.
She wanted to hear his voice, not a machine's. She
hung up and dialed his cell phone.

The line rang four times, and she was anticipating the call to roll into voice mail when he finally
answered. "Yes, Rei."

His tone of voice took her aback, but then again she shouldn't have expected a warm reception. She wasn't the only one who'd been hurt. Rei tightened her grip on the handset, but kept the tension out of her voice.

"Hi, Chris. How are you?"

"Fine, thanks. Was there something you wanted?"

You. I want you. "I'm calling to apologize. I wanted to let you know that I'm sorry and I hope you'll understand—"

"Of course. Giving up my nephew's case was just doing your job. I know that."

Rei smothered a hint of frustration. She knew he was upset, but still, this was not going as she'd hoped. She wasn't used to reaching out, and Chris wasn't making it any easier. Maybe it might be better to try to make amends in person.

"Are you doing anything this evening? We could meet somewhere for drinks."

He hesitated and she felt the silence grow into a barrier. When he finally spoke, his voice was colored with regret and sadness and resolve. "I don't think so. I don't have much of an appetite right now."

Rei closed her eyes, dropping her chin to her chest. Her heart constricted in denial even as her mind recognized the truth. His reference to the craving they'd felt from the beginning couldn't have been clearer. He wasn't hungry anymore. Not for her. Not for a woman who'd never given herself fully so that she wouldn't lose everything when it all went wrong.

Well, it had gone wrong anyway and she had only herself to blame. But she wasn't going to allow old hurt to keep getting in the way of new love. *Take a risk.*

"I—I miss you, Chris."

"I miss you, too. But I've gotten used to it." He sighed, a soft exhalation against the phone that said more than she wanted to hear. "You've been leaving me ever since we met and I'm not going to keep begging you to stay. I'm glad to know you're okay. I hope someday you'll be happy. Take care, Rei."

There was a click and then the buzz of the dial tone filled her ear. A lesser woman might have seen that as an ending. However, Rei wasn't about to give up on the best thing that had ever happened to her. Obviously it wasn't enough to say she was sorry, she knew that. So she'd have to find a way show him.

In her job, she gave people second chances all the time. Now she needed to give herself one and ask Chris to do the same.

"WE'LL BE BACK with The Bayside Morning Show *after these messages."*

Friday morning, Rei opened the doors to her closet while a commercial touted "quicker, thicker" paper towels. She rummaged through her clothes, agonizing over what to wear. She wasn't in the mood for her usual black, white or gray. It was a new day and she had a newfound determination to make it the best it could be.

"Welcome back to Bayside. I'm Autumn Matthews.

Our guests this morning are Eric Antoine, Michelle Johnson, Tina Farrell and Marvin Carrington."

Why had she bought that yellow dress? She looked awful in yellow. It was supposed to be decent weather today, so maybe she could wear the light-weight mint-green sweater....

"As you probably know, San Francisco's hottest dating service has recently come under fire for some questionable practices." Rei whipped her head around to stare at the television screen. *"These four Lunch Meetings clients are here to try to set the record straight."*

She sank down on the edge of the bed to watch the interview. The show's host seemed to focus on the earnest-looking man immediately to her right. Eric Antoine turned out to be one of the station's producers and Michelle Johnson was a news copy editor.

Eric explained that he'd been interested in Michelle for months, but had been too unsure of himself to approach her. He claimed that everything changed when he signed up for Lunch Meetings.

"I give full credit to Chris London for getting Michelle and I together. His courtship counseling forced me to take a deeper look at my life and the kind of woman I wanted to share it with."

"But, Eric," the host contended, *"the* Inquirer *article implied that the profile results were being manipulated. Don't you wonder how you and Michelle were paired up?"*

Michelle shook her head and smiled. *"Not at all.*

I never signed up for the service. So there's no way Chris could have messed around with our compatibility results."

Rei felt her face heat in shame. She'd believed the worst about Chris without ever giving him the benefit of the doubt. Her attitude had been small-minded and callous and unforgiving—everything she hated about her father.

On the show, Autumn cocked her head to one side. *"But he did offer you two, as well as other male clients, special additional services, right? And how much more did he charge for these clothes shopping trips and etiquette lessons?"*

"No more than I would have paid an image consultant, Autumn. I wasn't charged any outrageous fees, but frankly," Eric turned to look at Michelle and the affection is his gaze was obvious, *"the help Chris gave me was worth any price."*

The round-faced man next to Eric spoke up hesitantly. *"I know this is going to sound trite, but I think Chris does this out of the goodness of his heart."*

"Oh, come on, Marvin, you can't be serious?" asked Autumn.

When Tina leaned over to take his hand, he sat up a little straighter and looked the interviewer in the eye. *"If you read the Lunch Meetings literature carefully, there are no express guarantees that any client will end up in a relationship. The brochure only promises to introduce you to people who seem to be compatible."*

"Chris didn't have to coach the guys," Tina insisted. *"I think he saw their sincerity and loneliness and, if not for his advice, they wouldn't have had the confidence to enter a relationship."*

Michelle nodded. *"I have to admit, I wouldn't have given Eric a second chance except that I noticed the results of Chris's suggestions."*

Autumn turned to the other couple. *"Now, I understand you two just got engaged?"*

Tina beamed happily. *"Yes, we did. We're planning a winter wedding, and Chris's is the first name on our guest list. I've never been happier or more in love."*

Marvin blushed and cleared his throat. *"Let's face it, I'm not the best looking guy and I've always been shy. Chris identified and helped bring out my positive qualities, as well as coaching me on how to act more confidently. Thanks to the Lunch Meetings service, I've found the perfect woman. Tina loves me unconditionally for exactly who I am."*

Rei didn't hear the rest of the interview. She didn't need to. Unconditional love was the one thing she'd desperately wanted for the past twenty-five years. She closed her eyes as the image of her mother filled her mind and the memory of Keiko's love pervaded her heart.

Then another face appeared, the face of the man who'd offered wholehearted friendship and uninhibited passion. She was still hurt over his reaction to her cancer scare, but she knew from other women in her support group that friends and family, especially males, often responded negatively to hide their fear.

That was another example of her believing the worst of Chris without asking him to explain. Her ethics had been called into question twice recently. However, the Bayside interview had just reminded her of something very important. Ethics was as much about doing the right thing as about upholding the law.

Rei stood up and went back to the closet. She had to get dressed and get to the courthouse. She had a lot to do today.

13

Friday, April 25th

> Accomplishments: Perform an anonymous good deed; Ask for forgiveness; Tell someone you love them

"COMMISSIONER DAVIS, you're in early this morning. And you're… Pink."

Rei smiled at Mary Alice and twirled to show off her coral and white floral blouse and dark peony skirt. "I'm making a few changes."

Mary Alice nodded. "Change can be good. It keeps life interesting."

"What's on the docket for today?"

Her court services clerk thumbed through the files in her arm as she rattled off the morning's cases. "We've got a couple of divorces, an abuse case and several custody disputes."

"Another fun-filled day, huh?" She shoved her purse into one of the desk drawers. "Before we get started, I need to take care of a couple of things."

Mary Alice shifted the files again. "Sure, Commissioner. You've got about a half hour before I call the first case."

"Perfect." Rei picked up the phone and dialed P.J.'s number. She spun her desk chair toward the window, once again making a mental note to try the opera sometime soon. Her friend answered on the third ring.

"Hi, Peej. It's me. How's the Queen of the World today?"

"Hm, sounds like you're buttering me up for something. What's going on?"

"I need to talk to you about taking a risk."

Ten minutes later, she hung up the phone excited. P.J. had a good head for business and bottom lines, but she was also a romantic at heart. Rei knew she could be counted on to come through with this favor. She bounced out of her chair and prepared to ask for another one.

As she walked along the hallway, she came across the supervising judge, going the other way. "'Morning, Judge Orr."

His bushy white brows shot up in response to her outfit, but he nodded a greeting as he passed. "Commissioner."

Rei smiled to herself. Little did Judge Orr know that she was about to shoot his "zero-tolerance policy" straight to hell. She remembered how it was to be an emotionally neglected child, to feel unwanted and ignored. She knocked on the door to her friend Commissioner Whitney's chambers and stuck her head inside.

"Hi, Sarah. Have you got a moment? I'd like to discuss the Russo case."

THE AFTERNOON HAD dragged on endlessly, until finally Chris had made the decision to send Lara home early. The dining room had served fewer than a dozen people all day and it closed at three anyway. There hadn't been any potential new clients to meet, and he didn't have any private consultations tonight.

It was a situation that he might have to get used to unfortunately.

By four-thirty, Chris was pretty much alone. There were two people in the computer café, checking and sending e-mails, so he'd left the entrance doors unlocked. He sat in his office looking through his files, making a stack of the clients who had demanded either refunds or compensation so he could go over them with his accountant.

The short-term losses were going to seriously cut into his cash reserves. Long term? He had no idea what effect Grant Bronson's article would have. He'd truly appreciated Eric and Marvin's kind words on TV this morning, but he wasn't sure their endorsements would be enough.

Chris had to face the fact that he wasn't going to be able to expand Lunch Meetings anytime soon. He hadn't lost as many clients as he'd feared he might, nor had new applications fallen off significantly. But he'd have to wait out the negative publicity before he could start the venture capital process over again with another firm.

Although his parents had generously offered to put together some kind of loan and he'd been touched by the gesture, he was unwilling to let them take the risk. They had their own future to save for.

He'd thought, now that the dream of having his parents reunite had come true, the empty feeling in his chest would have gone away. Instead it felt as if it had grown. His mother had once cautioned him not to confuse success with fulfillment. Now that Rei was gone and the business was failing, what did he have? Nothing that mattered.

The e-mail program on his computer beeped, indicating he had a new message. His heart skipped a single beat when he saw who it was from.

TO: DCL3
FROM: RLDavis@email.com
SOMEONE LISTENED
Yesterday you said you wanted for someone to offer Gabriel a second chance. He's going to get one.
I spoke with the commissioner who'll be hearing Gabe's case. She will, of course, have to read the file and hear testimony from both sides. But she said she'd consider my suggestion of psychotherapy as well as family counseling. I don't know whether she'll be able to dismiss the charges, but at least Gabriel won't be facing incarceration.
Rei

As Chris read the last sentence a second time, his mouth curved into a smile. His sense of relief was indescribable. So his was surprise. After the way she'd spoken to him at the courthouse, he couldn't believe what she'd done and told her so.

RE: ACTING AS WELL AS LISTENING
I don't know what to say, Rei. I'm stunned and incredibly grateful. Thank you very much. Thank you on behalf of my family as well.
I hope your intervention won't cause you trouble at work.
Chris

RE: TROUBLE
I can trust Commissioner Whitney's discretion, though she was as surprised by my request as you are. Some people are worth the trouble, though, as you showed me yesterday. You stood up for your belief in Gabriel. I couldn't do any less.
Rei

RE: SECOND CHANCES
This means so much, Rei, but you know that. Thank you again.
Chris

RE: A FRIEND IN NEED
I'm not the kind of person who asks for what she needs. But that doesn't mean I don't need any-

thing. You once told me that the deep questions are the hardest to ask, but they're important. So I'm asking, will you give me another chance?
Rei

RE: DEEP QUESTIONS
We can talk about it, sure. Where are you now?
Chris

The security system magnet above the entrance buzzed. Chris turned to look through the two-way mirror to see who was coming in. As Rei walked through the door, she held up her text pager. She'd been just outside the whole time. He got up from his desk and went to meet her.

Late afternoon sunlight sparkled on her dark hair as she stood waiting for him. The pastel colors of her outfit added a soft femininity to her exotic looks, emphasizing her intelligent eyes and sensual mouth. He'd forgotten how beautiful she was, but not how much he loved her.

A sense of déjà vu hit him in the gut. The day she'd walked into Lunch Meetings, he'd claimed her as his own, just like he had on the dance floor at Divas. But, as she'd proven the last two times they'd seen each other, he had no more of her heart now than on that first day.

Rei offered him a tentative smile, obviously unsure of her welcome. "It's, uh, not very busy in here."

Chris's laugh was devoid of any humor. "It was

plenty busy on Monday when people started demanding their money back."

"I think it will be okay. Like you told me after the Grayson case, the media has a short attention span. Things will be back to normal soon."

"I hope you're right."

They looked at each other in awkward silence. Chris stuffed his hands into his pants pockets while Rei twisted the strap of her purse. He hated this. He wanted *everything* back to normal. No, that wasn't true. He wanted it to be better than before.

Her lips parted but it was another second before the words came. "I have a problem, Chris, and I'm hoping you can help me."

"I'll do my best."

"You always do, don't you?" She gave him a smile that didn't reach her eyes. "The problem is that Lunch Meetings matched me with the perfect guy. He's smart and sexy, passionate and caring. However the relationship has hit a barrier and I don't know what to do."

In Rei's chocolate brown eyes he saw his own insecurity reflected as well as a flash of longing. But he saw something else in her face, a kind of determined hope. He wanted to take her in his arms and hold her tight as his protective instincts kicked in at the sight of her vulnerability.

"I guess I wasn't really ready to find the love of my life." She took a step toward him and touched the back of his hand. "But I am now. We've shared things about our lives, but haven't had a lot of the open communication discussed in the Lunch Meetings brochure. So I've come to ask you for some court-ship counseling."

REI WANTED to work things out.

Chris instinctively turned his hand to grasp her fingers. The tiniest flame of hope began to melt the layer of ice that he'd wrapped around his heart when he'd thought they were through. "Why don't you go wait in my office while I show these clients out? I'll be right there."

He was as diplomatic as possible, but he still emptied the computer café in under a minute. The instant the front door closed behind his clients, he locked it and went to Rei. He walked into his office to find her standing nervously in the middle of the room. "Would you like to sit down?"

Rei shook her head and began to pace the floor, her footsteps muffled by the thick carpet. She'd taken off her coat and since she'd set her purse down, she was twisting her interlaced fingers instead. He didn't think he'd seen her so unsure of herself before.

"So, you'd like professional advice. I usually don't offer counseling unless I'm certain the client is genuinely interested in a lasting relationship…."

"You've given up on me." Rei's voice was no more than a grief-stricken whisper. She wrapped her arms about her waist, hanging her head.

Chris raked a hand through his hair. "I didn't give

up, Rei. I let go. It was crystal clear that, despite your agreeing to be more than lovers and becoming friends, you didn't want to risk letting me be a real part of your life."

She stopped before him and reached out to touch his arm. "That day Dr. Solís called—"

"Was one of the worst days of my life."

"I'm sorry. I looked at your face and immediately thought I saw rejection, so I rebuffed you first."

"How could you think I would turn away at a time like that? I wanted to be with you, to comfort and hold you…but you wouldn't let me near you." His voice broke and he looked away. "I thought, if you'd shut me out at a time like that, there's no hope of a future with you."

"I'm sorry, Chris, I really am. I've been so afraid to be vulnerable, to reach out only to have my hand slapped away, to trust anyone too far inside where they could hurt me."

He smiled sadly. "If you're looking for absolute assurances that you won't be hurt, you're looking in vain."

"I know that in my head, but in my heart… I've always assumed that because my father rejected me, because he's never been there for me, no one else would be either. So when I found the perfect guy, I blew it by being scared. I pushed you away because by caring, you'd have the power to hurt me the most."

He rested his hip on the edge of his desk and watched her cross the room again, his voice quiet. "Nobody's perfect, Rei, especially not me. You're not the only one to blame for things not working out. I've held myself back, too, never letting anyone inside because I knew they wouldn't stay. When you asked me to leave that afternoon—"

Rei touched her fingertips to his mouth, stopping his words. Her dark gaze compelled him to look into her eyes and see what was in her heart. There he saw tenderness and uncertainty and infinite depths of emotion. "There's something I need to tell you, Chris. But I'm a little afraid to, even now. I've never told any man this before in my life."

"You ought to know by now that you can tell me anything, that I won't judge you." When she still hesitated, he chuckled softly, pointing to his computer. "Do you want to type it into an e-mail and then step aside so I can read it?"

She laughed along with him and he saw some of the tension leave her, though her face was still set in serious lines of doubt. Rei took a breath and huffed it out again. "I'm not sure how you feel, but I love you, Chris. And I'm finally willing to risk being vulnerable, because I'm more afraid of losing you than I am of getting hurt."

Chris swallowed the lump in his throat. "Like I said before, there are no guarantees in relationships. But if I offer my heart, and all of the love I so badly want to give, and you walk away again, I don't think I'll ever get over the loss."

"I'm not asking you for any promises, Chris. I'm asking you for some time." Rei cupped his cheek in her palm and tipped his head until he met her gaze. Tears spilled from her eyes and her voice was hoarse with emotion. "Because time is the only way I can prove to you that I'm fully committed and that I'm not going to leave. I've spent so many years believing I wasn't worthy of love, convincing myself that I didn't need it in my life. But I do, Chris. I love you and I need you."

He felt the truth of her words touch him all the way to his soul. Maybe Jeanna was right and sometimes you just had to have faith. "I didn't get the chance to tell you—the man my mom's been dating is my dad."

She laughed in surprise. "You're kidding!"

"If they can work things out, so can we." He stood up and gathered her into his arms, knowing he'd never again let her go. "I love you, too, Rei, and I always will."

Rocking gently from side to side, he pressed his lips to her temple and stroked one hand over the dark silk strands of her hair. Rei reveled in the strength of his embrace, the warmth of his love and the emotional connection that she hoped would bind them to each other from now on.

She tightened her hold on him in happy silence, expressing by the purity of touch her joy at being together with him again. She felt as if time had stopped, like they'd never parted. Rei marveled at her newfound feelings of tenderness, intimacy and love. Chris had unlocked her heart with his quiet strength, integrity and courage.

He picked her up and turned so that she sat on his desk, putting their faces at a closer level. She slipped one arm behind his neck while he hugged her and nuzzled her cheek. Her other fingers skimmed his brow, touched his cheeks, traced the contours of his mouth. She placed her hand on the side of his face and pulled him forward until their lips met.

The kiss was warm, sweet and heartbreakingly tender. Chris tilted his head down and teased her lips apart with his tongue. She opened to him, to the tenderness of his slow, healing kiss, and slid her tongue over his in slow exploration. Heat, warm and penetrating, increased the need arcing between them until the kiss became eager and urgent.

Chris's big, hot hands pushed at the hem of her skirt, raising it to the apex of her thighs. Then he nudged her legs apart and pulled her to the edge of the desk. His mouth slanted over hers again, and again the kiss was raw and lusty and left her gasping for air. It was hard and hot and hungry and in less than a minute, so was he.

Desire sang in her blood as she felt the hard evidence of his lust through the thin cotton of her panties. She unbuttoned his shirt, kissing his jaw, the base of his throat and then his chest. Chris sought her mouth again and he kissed her wildly, passionately while she shoved the material off his shoulders.

The heavy throb of sexual need stirred in the pit of her stomach as she ran her hands over lean muscles of his bare back. She felt his skin heat beneath her roving hands and her own body ignited in response. Raw need built inside her as she captured his lips and explored his mouth in a hot, greedy kiss.

Chris broke away just long enough to strip her blouse from her. He unhooked her bra and cupped the weight of her breasts in his palms. His thumbs massaged the nipples to sensitive peaks, then he bent his head to take one into his mouth. When he began suckling gently, she exhaled a sharp gasp of pleasure at the wet, tugging sensation.

Her hands raked through his hair, holding his head in place as he gave her other breast the same attention. Rei arched her back and groaned as white-hot bolts of lust shot through her body. Dampness pooled in her feminine center and her vaginal muscles began to quiver with need.

When Chris reluctantly moved away from her to finish taking off his pants, she slid off the desk so she could unzip her skirt and step out of it. Her bra and panties quickly followed, then she looked up to admire his naked body. Desire overwhelmed her in a powerful rush. She wanted him. Very badly.

He magically produced a condom from somewhere, then reached for her. He gently guided her down onto the soft pile carpet, kneeling beside her to once again claim her mouth. She lay back and held her arms out to him. After making sure they were protected, he moved over her and positioned himself between her legs.

She reached between their bodies to take his throbbing penis in her hand. Gliding her fingers along the length of his shaft, she spread her thighs and guided him into her wet passage. Her body clenched, then adjusted and welcomed him as he slowly filled her to the hilt.

Her sigh of pleasure quickly transformed into a moan of desire. Chris smiled at her and held her gaze. Love shown in his eyes as he worshipped her body in the most intimate way. She skimmed her hands along his sides until she cupped his taut buttocks and urged him closer, deeper.

He accelerated the tempo, surging forward and pulling back only to plunge into her again, harder and deeper. Wrapping her legs tighter around his hips, her hands clutched at the sweat slick muscles of his back. The relentless pressure in her womb increased until the orgasm shuddered through her, rocking her to the core.

An eternity later Chris's body tensed and she could feel the deep pulsating in his shaft that signaled his climax. The contractions ripped a cry from his throat and he pressed his face to her shoulder to muffle the sound. Her body was still clenching with the aftereffects of amazing sex when he finally withdrew and shifted his weight off of her.

They lay side by side, sweating, while Rei tried to catch her breath and slow her heart rate. After a moment, Chris got up and went into the small washroom. He eventually came back and handed her a warm cloth and a dry towel before turning away to find his briefs.

"So, sweetheart, what do you want to do for the rest of the evening?"

"I want to go home, Chris. I want to hold you all night long and rejoice in knowing you'll be there when I wake up in the morning and every morning after that. Then, tomorrow, I've got a very special lunch meeting."

Saturday, April 26th

Accomplishments: Jump out of a plane on purpose

"OH, MY GOD! Are we really going to do this?" Rei shouted to be heard, not an easy task when the thin air made it hard to breathe and the whine of the propellers droned in her ears.

Chris grinned at her from beneath the protective goggles covering his eyes. "We're almost at ten thousand feet. It's a little late to be asking that."

"I can still change my mind though, right?"

"Not if you want to check this off your List."

Her stomach had started fluttering as they'd driven out of the city this morning, heading north on Highway 12. It had continued to quiver throughout meeting her tandem instructor, watching the safety video and completing the brief training class. Now, during the agonizingly slow climb to the fifteen thousand feet, her stomach was downright quaking.

All too soon, the plane reached the jump ceiling and it was time to jump. Her instructor tapped her on the shoulder. "Are you ready to fly?"

Rei gave him a shaky thumbs-up. While he connected their harnesses, she watched Chris and his tandem disappear through the open doorway of the plane. *Oh, God. Am I really going to do this?* In less time than she would have liked, her instructor was holding her and leaping out into empty space. They tumbled once, twice, and then began freefalling.

Her heart thundered in her chest as her stomach tried to join it. The noise was unbelievably loud despite her helmet and the wind shear chilled her even wearing the heavy coveralls. She was hurtling through the air at over 120 miles per hour and screaming herself hoarse. She'd never felt so scared and exhilarated at the same time.

With a sudden, hard jerk, the parachute deployed and almost instantly there was silence. Her heart still pounded, but now it was from the sheer thrill of floating and gliding though the sky. Rei felt tears sting her eyes. There was no way she'd ever be able to describe this sense of peace combined with pure adrenaline rush.

At the sound of Chris howling like a crazed wolf, she looked up to see a huge grin plastered across his face. At this moment, she couldn't love him more. Rei laughed out loud, a heartfelt genuine sound of joy and triumph. *This is for you, Miriam. And for me and for the rest of my life.*

Epilogue

A COOL OCTOBER BREEZE drifted through the open front door of Lunch Meetings' newest branch, alleviating some of the heat that resulted from packing so many bodies into one place.

The large storefront windows overlooked the night skyline of downtown Oakland. A string quartet played in one corner, though the murmur and hum of conversation competed with the music. Silver candelabra glowed on tables set with creamy white linen and tall vases of scarlet roses with tiny white sprays of baby's breath.

Waiters in white dinner jackets offered trays of hors d'oeuvres to the fifty or so clients and reporters milling about. Two cameramen circulated through the gathering, capturing the event on film, while Autumn Matthews conducted interviews for a later broadcast on her Bayside Morning Show.

Rei stood with P.J., sipping champagne and watching from across the lobby while Chris shook Eric Antoine's hand. He turned as another man clapped him on the back and engaged him in conversation. She thought he was engrossed in what the man was saying until Chris suddenly looked right at her and smiled.

Rei grinned in response then turned to her best friend, who had gone toe to toe with her father's cronies in order to get Chris the venture capital. "Thanks again for making this happen."

P.J. shrugged gracefully, causing the pashmina wrap to slip off her shoulders. "All I did was authorize the money. Chris is the one who makes Lunch Meetings a success. It was a smart investment."

"Have you gotten used to being completely in charge of Hollinger/Hansen yet?"

"No. I think I'm still a little shocked." Unbeknownst to P.J., there had been a codicil to her father's will stating that if she ever dismissed the Board of Directors, she was to be named CEO and Chairperson with full authority to make decisions for the company.

"I guess Kent had a lot more faith in you than you realized." Rei smiled and touched her flute to P.J.'s in a toast. "Here's to facing down our insecurities."

After draining her glass and handing it to a passing waiter, P.J. moved off to mingle. "I think that hot looking guy over there might need financial planning advice."

Rei was content to stand on the sidelines while the guests nibbled Brie and Bosc pears, chatted with the media and attempted to dance. It was difficult to hear the music, but looking at Marvin Carrington and his fiancée Tina Farrell, it was obvious they were swaying to their own tune anyway.

Suddenly Rei felt a pair of hands slide down her arms while a familiar pair of lips pressed a kiss to her temple. Chris slowly twirled her around, admiring her red satin cocktail dress and matching heels. "You look beautiful tonight, sweetheart."

Rei gave him an exaggerated once-over, taking in the sight of him in his white linen shirt and tuxedo. "You're looking rather spectacular yourself."

"You both look gorgeous!" She turned around to see Autumn Matthews and her cameraman. "Can I ask you a few questions as a couple? Great! Okay, roll in three, Larry."

Autumn quickly held up a small microphone. "So, Rei, Chris, how long have the two of you been together now?"

Chris smiled but left it to her to answer. "A little over five months."

"And what would you say is the secret to your obvious happiness?"

Rei had been quietly promoting the dating service for a while now and so was prepared for the question. "The key is in determining the vital attributes that are important to you and then discovering compatible core traits in your partner. That's what allows us to connect on a deeper level. That philosophy is integral to how Lunch Meetings works and we're proof of the results."

Autumn came back with a follow-up question. "Okay, so much for the corporate hard sell. Wouldn't you admit that it takes more than a digital database to get two people together?"

Chris spoke up. "That's very true, Autumn. Finding a lasting relationship is more than statistical probability and orchestrated opportunity. At some point, you have to throw logic out the window and take a leap of faith."

Autumn positioned the mike in front of Rei. "Would you agree with that?"

Rei looked up, smiled at Chris and saw the depth of his love reflected in his light-green gaze. She knew that hadn't always been his philosophy. Nor hers for that matter. Their being together owed as much to coincidence, fate and magic as to the Lunch Meetings computer software.

She snuggled against Chris's side when he kissed her cheek. "Yes, absolutely. I've finally found the love of my life."

If you enjoyed what you just read,
then we've got an offer you can't resist!

Take 2 bestselling love stories FREE!

Plus get a FREE surprise gift!

▨▨▨▨▨▨▨▨▨▨▨▨▨▨▨▨▨▨▨▨▨

Clip this page and mail it to Harlequin Reader Service®

IN U.S.A.	**IN CANADA**
3010 Walden Ave.	P.O. Box 609
P.O. Box 1867	Fort Erie, Ontario
Buffalo, N.Y. 14240-1867	L2A 5X3

YES! Please send me 2 free Harlequin® Blaze™ novels and my free surprise gift. After receiving them, if I don't wish to receive anymore, I can return the shipping statement marked cancel. If I don't cancel, I will receive 6 brand-new novels each month, before they're available in stores! In the U.S.A., bill me at the bargain price of $3.99 plus 25¢ shipping and handling per book and applicable sales tax, if any*. In Canada, bill me at the bargain price of $4.47 plus 25¢ shipping and handling per book and applicable taxes**. That's the complete price and a savings of at least 10% off the cover prices—what a great deal! I understand that accepting the 2 free books and gift places me under no obligation ever to buy any books. I can always return a shipment and cancel at any time. Even if I never buy another book from Harlequin, the 2 free books and gift are mine to keep forever.

151 HDN D7ZZ
351 HDN D72D

Name	(PLEASE PRINT)
Address	Apt.#
City	State/Prov. Zip/Postal Code

Not valid to current Harlequin® Blaze™ subscribers.

Want to try two free books from another series?
Call 1-800-873-8635 or visit www.morefreebooks.com.

* Terms and prices subject to change without notice. Sales tax applicable in N.Y.
** Canadian residents will be charged applicable provincial taxes and GST.
All orders subject to approval. Offer limited to one per household.
® and ™ are registered trademarks owned and used by the trademark owner and/or its licensee.

BLZ05   ©2005 Harlequin Enterprises Limited.